the Lamp

ABBY BURCH

Copyright © 2018 Abby Burch

All rights reserved.

Trademarks used herein are owned by their respective trademark owners and are used without permission.

No part of this publication may be reproduced in whole or in part, or stored in a retrieval system, or transmitted in any form or by any means, electronic, mechanical, photocopying, recording, or otherwise, without written permission of the author.

This is a work of fiction. Any and all likenesses to real people or events are purely coincidental.

ISBN: 9781723743702

For Taz,
The world's best cuddle buddy.

1. BRENNA

"Come on, it's going to be fun," my roommate/best friend Carly whines at me while dragging a flat iron down her long, dark brown hair.

"I know," I sigh as I trudge out of the jack-and-jill bathroom separating our bedrooms and open my closet door. "It's just hard to be excited for your engagement when I'm probably going to be alone forever." I start rifling through my closet for something nice to wear. Carly and John have been dating for over two years now, and she's the last of our friend circle to get engaged.

Besides me, that is.

"Bren, you're a smart, beautiful woman, and any guy would be lucky to have you," Carly calls out from the bathroom.

She's not wrong, it's just that for the past decade, there's only been one guy that I've wanted. And unfortunately, he doesn't want me.

I'm moving on from Ashton, for real this time.

Unfortunately, I'm not really sure what that means for me quite yet... but for now, I'm going to be supportive of Carly and John, and try not to be a bitter old hag.

I quickly throw my favorite black dress over my head and smooth the fabric down my body. It has short sleeves, with a sheer panel across the upper chest that gives just a hint at my cleavage, and the waist hits at just the right spot into a flared bottom, giving the illusion of a more curvy figure than I actually have. It's my go-to dress because not only does it fit me perfectly, but it is also ultra-comfortable.

I hear the front door open in the distance and a voice calls out, "Are you guys almost ready?"

"In a minute, John!" Carly yells back at her fiancé from the bathroom. I'm slipping a silver bangle bracelet onto my wrist as John pokes his head into my room from the bathroom to wave hello.

John is perfect for Carly. Not just because he's incredibly handsome, but because he's the yin to her yang. As crazy and spontaneous as she is, he's laid back, cool and collected. Also, he's always been nice to me and not just to impress his girlfriend's best friend to get her approval or anything - John is just truly a nice guy and we've become good friends as a result of his relationship with Carly.

"Thanks for arranging everything tonight, Brenna," he says to me with a genuine smile.

"Of course," I reply, turning to my full length mirror for a once-over. "As the Maid of Honor, it's my honor to do it."

Soon enough, the three of us are out the door and arriving at the restaurant for the first part of the evening. It's a higher-end place and was at the top of my budget, but it's one of Carly's favorite places, and is where she and John had their first date, so it was an obvious choice for a celebratory dinner with friends.

Our reserved table is in one of the back rooms. We quickly settle in and Carly cracks into the wine as the rest of her friends begin to arrive. She pours me a small glass, knowing that wine isn't my jam but I'll suffer through it when needed, and we share a silent toast with a smile.

Carly's social circle is much larger than mine. People naturally gravitate to her - she's gorgeous, funny, and a social butterfly. Of course, all of these people could be considered my friends as well, however I prefer to call the majority of them acquaintances as I'm not close with most of them. Carly and John are my only real close "friends" any more, partly of my own choosing and partly because of Ashton.

Dinner is fabulous, and John and Carly are having a blast. Seeing Carly so happy would be enough to lift anyone out of a funk, so it's impossible for me to be a party pooper, even though I'm by far the most sober person in the room.

As things are winding down, I head up to the hostess podium to pay the remainder of what I owe for the evening. I'm pretty sure I hear my poor Amex cry in pain as they slide it through the card reader. I don't have a choice though - as a twenty-seven year old college grad who will probably be paying on my student loans until I'm eighty, American Express has unfortunately become a close friend, except at places where they don't accept American Express. Luckily I also have my friends Visa and MasterCard as backup.

I know it isn't a good plan or responsible to rely on credit cards, but for now, it's either that or default on my student loans and have it come back on my family who co-signed for them. And I can't let that happen, no matter what.

As I return to the table, Carly excitedly tells me that we're going barhopping from here. She's already pretty drunk, which only makes her want to party harder. I groan and try to protest, but she cuts me off. "Come on, Bren! Let's go have some fun. We deserve it."

"That's what you say every time we go out," I mumble half-heartedly. She doesn't hear it though because she's already halfway out the door, along with most of our dinner group.

The bar is packed and it takes a while for all 15 of us to be able to get in. Carly and several of the other girls immediately go secure one of the large round tables near the back while the guys go to get drinks. I plop down next to Carly and scope out the scene. The table we picked is near the dance floor, so my eyeballs are immediately bombarded by some really terrible drunken dance moves being performed by a couple of college-age guys. At least the DJ tonight seems to be decent.

John and the guys show up with a couple pitchers of beer and two rounds of shots for all of us. Reluctantly, I down the shots I'm given and immediately feel the warmth hit all of my insides. I really planned on staying mostly-sober tonight, but now I'm reconsidering. After all, I can always catch an Uber home.

The DJ is pumping some dance tunes, and soon enough, Carly is dragging me to the dance floor. I'm not a dancer, but she's a natural along with several of her friends, so they begin moving fluidly to the beat while I awkwardly shuffle. Some of the guys join us as well, and dance with their fiancées/wives.

I watch John and Carly dancing together, so lost in each other, and I feel the knife of jealousy twisting in my stomach. I try so hard to ignore its presence, but sometimes it is easier than others. I can't say that I've ever been as happy as Carly is right now. I honestly can't say I've been even *close* to as happy as she is when she's with John.

I can't seem to catch my breath and I realize I'm about to have a panic attack. A jealousy-induced panic attack – great. I immediately escape the dance floor and head to the bar. I need to get out of my own head, so I catch the attention of the bartender and order my favorite shot - Sex with an Alligator.

"You're going to have sex with an alligator?" A male voice next to me says incredulously. I turn to look at the source of the question and am greeted by the most gorgeous blue eyes I've ever seen in my entire life. They're such a light shade of blue that they remind me of the wispy clouds that drift across the sky on a warm summer day.

The bearer of aforementioned eyes is close to a foot taller than I am, which at 5'4" isn't exactly common but isn't unheard of, either. He has dark hair, cut short on the sides and longer on top, gelled upwards into a gravity-defying style. His beard is short and well-groomed, and he's sporting a smirk.

"Well, of course," I try to say as smoothly as possible. "When you're having a shitty night, the best way to make it better is to have sex with a dangerous, wild animal."

The guy laughs, and it might be the sexiest sound I've ever heard. I may be mistaken though, as my head is pounding along with the techno beat that is thundering through the bar.

"So that's how you fix a shitty night, huh?" He says as he turns to the bartender and shouts to make it two shots. By some miracle the bartender actually hears the guy over the music and begins to make a second shot.

"I'm Ryan, by the way," he says, extending his hand toward mine.

"Brenna," I say, and give his hand a firm shake. I feel a surge of energy pass between us. I quickly pull my hand away and clear my throat. Luckily, the bartender comes back with our shots at that moment. Ryan tells him to put them both on his tab.

He holds up his shot, which is tri-colored layers of deliciousness, and says "to improving shitty nights by having sex with deadly animals."

"Cheers," I clink his glass with a grin.

Three shots later, my cheeks are tingly and the room is starting to spin. Ryan is proving to be quite a conversationalist, and I'm actually enjoying myself. Briefly, I've forgotten that I'm 15th-wheeling my best friend's engagement party and I let myself get sucked into Ryan's eyes. And smile. And mild accent - possibly Canadian? And his presence in general.

Maybe it's the alcohol talking, but I'm feeling unusually bold. "So what brings you out tonight?" I ask him.

It's gone as quickly as it was there - some kind of dark flash behind Ryan's eyes. If I hadn't been so entranced by them, I would have missed it. It is instantly replaced by the playful sparkle that had been there before. "I knew there would be a beautiful girl at this bar tonight that I needed to get to know."

My cheeks burn even more. He's flirting, and I'm drunk, and I'm jealous and pissed off that everyone around me is happy in long term relationships, and he's so insanely hot that I can barely believe he's talking to me, let alone flirting.

"You're adorable when you blush, Brenna," he says to me, his voice velvety smooth. My heart pounds in my chest along with the music.

The alcohol has lowered my inhibitions and apparently my filter as well. "You're sexy as hell," I attempt to flirt back, immediately realize what I have said, and clap a hand over my mouth. Luckily, Ryan laughs as he puts his arm around my waist. My body reacts to the touch and goosebumps immediately ricochet across my arms. There's an undercurrent of electricity flowing between us.

So when Ryan leans in and whispers in my ear, "Want to get out of here?" I nod.

I'm not a one night stand kind of girl. But you know what? Fuck it. Tonight, I am.

2. RYAN

I walk with Brenna to the Uber waiting for us in front of the bar and hold the door open for her, ushering her inside. She stumbles slightly as she gets in. I slide in next to her and hand her the bottle of water I bought as we were getting ready to head out.

"Drink up," I say to her. "Hydration is important."

"Okay," she says with a smile and takes a swig. I keenly watch her perfect lips as she pulls the bottle away and licks the excess water from them. Fuck, she's so hot and I'm already sporting a semi. I need her to be at least somewhat sober, so I'm going to push water on her. I don't know how one shot turned into three, but it did. I didn't expect her to agree to come home with me, but she did.

Tonight is a night of unexpected surprises, that's for sure.

We pull up to the house and I give the driver a five-star rating before hopping out. I offer my hand to Brenna, who stands up much more steadily than she did when we left the bar. I guide her up the sloped driveway to the large, sprawling home in this new development in the suburbs. All of the houses are a little too new for my taste - I prefer the old, worn-in wood as opposed to that fake wood shit they put in most new developments now, but with the time crunch I was in, I'll take what I can get. It beats sleeping in a hotel.

Brenna's eyes are wide, the accent lights lining the front bushes reflecting off them. "Your house is huge," she says breathlessly.

"Thanks," I say nonchalantly as I unlock the front door and usher her into the foyer. It's got one of the two stairways to the second floor, plus there is a balcony that overlooks the foyer. I kick off my shoes and pad into the kitchen. "Are you hungry?"

"No, thank you," she says quietly, and I immediately sense nerves in her voice. She's standing near the kitchen island, wringing the bottom of her dress with trembling hands. It would bother me that she's nervous except that she's unintentionally lifting the front of her dress up slightly, revealing more of her slender legs.

"You haven't done a random hookup before, have you?" I ask. She shakes her head no, eyes at the floor. Damn if she isn't the sweetest thing. "Listen, you don't have to do anything you don't want to do."

She responds by launching herself at me and I'm stunned speechless by 115 lbs of beautiful woman kissing me. Her mouth is soft but urgent; she sears me as her tongue slides across my lips, begging me to let her in.

I hold the back of her head with one hand as the kiss deepens, my other hand pulling her waist into me. My dick presses uncomfortably against my jeans. I don't think she can feel it yet, but she will soon enough. Her hands glide up and down my back sending ripples through me.

"Brenna," I grit out, and she stares up at me with those big brown eyes. She reminds me of a doe in the cold Canadian snow, full of wide-eyed curiosity and innocence. "I want to fuck you. Is that okay?"

She nods with determination. "I would like that very much."

"Good," I say, then swiftly lift her up and over my shoulder. She squeals with a mixture of surprise and delight as I carry her down the hall and into the master bedroom.

Somewhat roughly, I toss her onto the bed, enjoying the view a little too much when her legs spread open and I see her bright pink underwear.

I pull my shirt over my head and throw it across the room onto the floor and Brenna gasps. I watch as her eyes roam over my body, taking in my six-pack abs. Being a professional athlete means I'm in great shape but it also means I'm highly recognizable. Thankfully, I don't think she knows who I am, which honestly makes things easier for both of us.

"Take off your dress," I command her, and she quickly sheds the garment. I take in the sight of her slim figure. All the best pieces are hidden by her pink underwear and black bra. Her slender stomach is toned, smooth, pale skin. Her blonde hair sits in light waves across her shoulders and chest, and she looks angelic.

Too bad she's dancing with the devil tonight.

I climb on top of her and press myself against her, holding most of my weight up on my arms as I meet her lips again. Her hips buck and grind against me and holy shit - I don't know what it is about this girl but if I don't calm down I'll embarrass myself, teenager style. It's only been a little over a week since I last got some pussy, so it's not like it's been an extraordinarily long amount of time or anything.

Brenna's hands slide up and down my arms, which are covered in tattoos. I finally finished my right sleeve earlier in the summer, so I'm covered in ink from shoulder to wrist on both arms.

I trail kisses down her jawbone, to her neck and down to her chest. We lock eyes and I wait for her permission to continue. I may be a bit of a man-whore at times, but I'd like to think I'm still a gentleman. I'll never push a girl farther than she'd like to go. She smiles and nods, giving me the go-ahead and

I slip my hands around her back, undoing the clasp on her bra in one quick motion.

Bra quickly discarded, I let my hands go to work. She moans as I palm her tits, her nipples tight under my hands. Brenna's boobs aren't huge but they're natural and that's more important to me than giant, fake tits. I take one nipple into my mouth and roll my tongue around it, teasing her, and the moan I get in response eggs me on. She moves her hands up into my hair and grips it tightly as I gently suck on her.

My jeans are now strangling my cock so I quickly dismount her and pull them off, along with my socks. My dick is at full attention inside my boxer-briefs, pointing straight toward the prize, and her beautiful, wide eyes are locked on it.

"Are you still sure you want to do this?"

"Ryan," she says breathily. It's so sexy. "Please, fuck me."

She doesn't have to tell me twice.

3. BRENNA

The heat in Ryan's eyes is carnal. He's immediately on top of me again, our mouths a tangle of lips and tongues, and his dick resting hotly against me. His hand glides across my collarbone and down my side, gripping my side as he grinds against me. Involuntarily, my hips buck, increasing the friction between us. Thankfully, Ryan grabs my panties and shimmies them down my legs, chucking them across the room. His red boxer-briefs quickly follow.

I'm not a prude, but I'm definitely not a hussy, either. I've only seen a handful of dicks in my lifetime, but none of them were as big or as beautiful as Ryan's. He keeps things well-maintained which shows off the incredible length and girth all the more, not that it needs any help.

He looks delectable and impossibly sexy. I'm feeling a little intimidated and a lot self-conscious. I haven't been keeping up on the downstairs maintenance very well because it's been out of service for so damn long. Ryan doesn't seem to mind though as he lays on his stomach in between my legs, tossing them over his shoulders.

Beginning at my knee, he starts trailing kisses along the inside of my thigh. It tingles and I feel a low burn of need in my belly, a moan escaping me as he plants a gentle kiss directly on my clit. He glances up at me and all I can see are his eyes, but that's all I need to see - they're dancing with desire.

I feel his tongue circling me and my vision clouds with stars. I clench my legs around his head, probably suffocating him but I'm on my way to cloud nine. He tongue-fucks me as one hand works my clit and instantly I'm propelled into an earth-shattering orgasm. It feels like I'm a star in supernova as every nerve ending in my body explodes at once.

Ryan barely lets my breathing slow before he's crawling up beside me, his hands caressing my bare skin. "You were spectacular," he says with a smile. Then his hand drifts back down the length of my body, sliding one finger easily between my slick folders and into me. I can't help it - a moan escapes me.

He inserts another finger and begins to pump them slowly while nibbling on my neck. I gingerly slide a hand down his chiseled chest and across what can literally be described as washboard abs. I thought men like this only existed in movies, magazines, and porn, but here I am, about to have sex with the hottest guy I have ever seen. His stomach is flat with rippling muscles, and even that coveted V shape leading down to the prize. I let my hand explore its way down until I'm gripping his dick. He growls from deep in his throats and I know he's as turned on as I am.

I slide my hand up and down his shaft in rhythm with him moving his hand in and out of me. He gently moves his hips into my hand in rhythm as our breathing quickens.

Abruptly, he pulls his fingers out of me, and I hold back a whimper from the loss of contact.

"I think you're ready for me," he says, slightly out of breath. He leans over to his bedside table and pulls a condom from the drawer. In a flash, he has the wrapper open and rolls the rubber onto his dick. "But, I'm not going to be gentle." He positions himself on top of me, rubbing his sheathed dick against my folds, teasing. I shudder with excitement. I have no second guessings now - I want him inside me, fucking me senseless.

I want to forget that I haven't gotten laid in almost a year.

I want to forget that my last fuck was Ashton, before I found out he had a fiancée back in Texas.

I want to forget that all my friends are in love and happy and I'm still pining after a guy who is no good for me.

I want to forget.

Ryan slides inside in one swift motion, pushing in all the way until I'm filled with him and I gasp at the sudden fullness. He waits there a moment, the calm before the storm. Then he begins to move, dragging himself almost all the way out before pushing back in to the hilt on each pass. I tangle my fingers in his hair as he somehow props himself up in such a way that he's able to play with my nipple with one hand as he continues to thrust. It's the most amazing sensation and my body is going haywire on sensory overload.

I quickly feel myself approaching the edge again, the burn in my belly dropping down into me and my hands balling into fists, gripping the grey sheets beneath me. "Ryan, I-I'm going to come." This information causes him to go into overdrive, all gentleness gone as he holds both of my shoulders and pounds vigorously into me. My head knocks into the headboard but it barely registers.

As I hit the peak, I cry out, the orgasm shattering me into a million pieces.

"Oh fuck, fuck, fuck," Ryan peaks a moment later, his thrusts becoming haphazard and unrhythmic as he spends himself inside me. He collapses partially on top of me, his dick still inside, panting heavily.

Every nerve in my body is ablaze. My bones are wet noodles and my brain is egg drop soup.

As our breathing slows and the blood returns to my brain from my vagina, I start to realize what I've just done.

I had sex with a complete and total stranger, a guy I met at the bar. This isn't Brenna behavior. I've always been a good girl - straight A's in high school and college, never skipped school or called in sick in my life, and definitely never had a one night stand.

I feel sick.

Ryan dislodges from me, fumbling around to remove the condom and tie it off. He tosses it into the wastebasket next to his bed with his eyes half-closed, which is kind of impressive.

Then I remember he's probably done that a thousand times and it suddenly isn't impressive anymore.

He shuts off the light on the nightstand and puts a heavily muscled and tattooed arm over me, pulling me closer to him.

He's asleep within 30 seconds, lightly snoring into my ear.

I just had sex with a stranger. A very hot stranger, but a stranger nonetheless. I feel the panic bubbling up, my throat constricting. I can't stay in his house for a single moment longer. Carefully, I pry his arm from me and he rolls over, spreading out across the bed. I make sure his breathing is still steady before I slide off the side of the bed.

It's dark, so I claw around the floor, find my underwear and slide them on. I find my dress in a crumpled heap across the room and pull it on over my head. My bra is nowhere to be found. I wonder if it possibly ended up under the bed but I'd rather cut my losses, get lost and forget this ever happened.

Ryan's chest rises and falls rhythmically. He's starfished out on the bed, none the wiser. I tiptoe out of his room and down the hall. Luckily, he left the kitchen light on, and I find my purse sitting on the kitchen counter next to a giant gym bag. I grab my purse, pulling my phone out and discover I have 17 texts and 31 missed calls from Carly. Shit, I never even told her I was leaving the bar or where I'd be. I don't even bother to read any of the messages or listen to the voicemails, I just immediately dial her and she picks up on the first ring.

"Where in the hell are you!?" She yells. I hear John in the background asking if it's me but she ignores him. "We have been looking all over for you. What the fuck, Bren!?"

"I'm sorry, Carls," I whisper as I walk to the foyer, where I thankfully find both of my shoes. "I, um, I forgot to tell you I was leaving."

"Yeah, no shit," she says sarcastically. "I figured that one out. Are you okay? Where are you?"

I peek out the front door of Ryan's house. All I see are street lights lining the cul-de-sac. "Um, I don't know, but I'll just get an Uber home."

"You don't know where you are!?" Carly screeches. "What happened? We are coming to find you."

"I'm okay," I whisper. "I will meet you at the house, okay?"

"Are you sure you're okay?" She is much more calm now.

I'm not sure I'm okay, but I can't tell her that right now. Not while I'm still in this house. "I'll be okay. I'll be there soon. Love you, Carls."

"Love you too. See you soon." She hangs up and I quickly pull up Uber and signal for a car to come here. I see based on the map that I'm in an outer suburb of Chicago, quite a long ride from home. Luckily, it's mid-September and the nights are still moderately warm, so I quietly slip out the door, it clicking closed behind me, and step out into the muggy late-summer night.

I walk down the driveway to the edge of the road, noticing that I'm sore in places I forgot could BE sore, and sit down on the edge of the curb.

The tears prick at my eyes, and I let them fall. I deserve every last one of them.

4. RYAN

The alarm blares, far too early. I bang my hand on it until it finally stops. Yawning, I stretch my arms over my head, noticing I'm completely naked. I usually sleep in boxer-briefs, so waking up naked is unusual for me.

Then I notice that the room smells like sex, and last night comes charging back into my mind. Blonde haired, brown eyed, petite, beautiful Brenna. Last night was pretty damn great. Although I only remember fucking her once. Usually I can bang three or four times in a single night before I'm too tired to function, but apparently I was exhausted last night.

I roll out of bed and pull on my boxer-briefs from the floor to go look for her. I check in both bathrooms on the main floor but they're empty. She isn't in the kitchen or living room either. I notice her purse and shoes are gone and deduct that she must have slipped out at some point. Too bad, because she was a lot of fun.

I head back to the master bathroom to take a quick shower. Today is my first practice with my new team, the Chicago Velocity. I was traded during the offseason after a lackluster season with the Philadelphia Drivers. I had been with them for seven years, ever since I was drafted into the league at 18.

I already have all my gear packed and ready to go in the kitchen, so as I go to shut the door to my bedroom, my hand touches silk.

Brenna's black bra is hanging from the doorknob in my bedroom. One of three things must have happened. Either

1) she left it there on purpose,

2) she couldn't find it, or

3) she was in such a haste to leave that she didn't care if it was left behind.

The first option is something a puck bunny would do. Puck bunny is a popular term in the hockey world for slutty girls who try to sleep with the players. They like to leave souvenirs as much as they like to take souvenirs. It also gives them a reason to come back around, hoping for a repeat performance. Brenna isn't a puck bunny and that doesn't feel like it's her style, so I rule out option one.

That leaves options two and three. I'm hoping she left it because she couldn't find it and not because she was insanely desperate to get away from me.

I don't know why I care so much. She was a one night stand in a new city. I'll never see her face again.

Yet, as I run my thumb across the silk bra in my hand, I can't help but want to run into her again.

I toss the garment on my bed as a reminder to look her up online after practice.

The captain of my new team, Patrick Huff, invites me out to lunch after morning skate. He seems like a nice enough dude. He's been captain of the Velocity for only a couple years, but we were drafted into the NHL the same year. He's a center, and I'm a wing, so there's a high probability that we'll end up playing on the same line at some point.

We head to a small bar called Two Bits Pub, located near the arena. Patrick must be a regular here because the waitress brings him a beer only a moment after we've sat down. She takes my drink order and bustles away to the bar without a second glance. The other patrons don't even look our way, which is unusual for someone of our celebrity.

"So, welcome to Chicago," Patrick says. "I know you've been with Philly since you were drafted, so it's a big change to come to Chicago, but I think you'll like it here."

"I'm looking forward to being here," I say earnestly. I'm still on guard though – I don't know if he's mentioning my being traded as a way to remind me of my piss-poor performance last season and put me in my place on my new team. I decide to believe he just wants to connect with the "new guy," mostly because I need to make a good first impression. If I mess things up in the next few weeks, I'll get sent down to the "farm team," which is the minor leagues and where old veterans go to watch their careers die. I know I'm better than the minors, but I have to prove it.

The waitress drops off my beer, takes our order, and heads back to the kitchen. She's average height but athletically built, with her dark hair cut short, hanging around her chin. I only ogle her a little before turning my full attention back to Patrick.

He gives me some background on the other guys on the team. I've played against most of them here and there, but since Chicago and Philly are in different conferences, I don't know them very well. Patrick also asks me about myself, from what I like most about hockey to what my favorite video game is. By the end of lunch, I'm feeling much more comfortable and I can see Patrick and I becoming real friends.

The waitress stops by and Patrick hands her his card. "I've got them both today, Morgan."

"Sure thing, Pat," she says and turns away to run the card. She's got a great ass. Apparently I'm staring, because Patrick clears his throats and says "That's my little sister."

Shit. "She seems very nice," I quickly say, running a hand through my hair. "Are you guys from Chicago originally?"

"Nah," Patrick says, seemingly forgetting that I was just checking out his sister. "We're from Minnesota, actually. Morgs moved here a couple years ago after our dad died."

"Shit, man. I'm sorry to hear that," I offer.

"Yeah. It's alright. Morgs and I have always been close, so it just made sense for her to move here. Plus it was a fresh start for her." Morgan comes back over to us and our conversation ceases. She hands Patrick the card and receipts and smiles at us.

"It was nice to meet you, Ryan," she says to me, her eyes full of platonic kindness. "I'm sure you're going to be a great addition to the Velocity's roster this year."

"Thank you. It was nice to meet you as well, Morgan." I shake her hand, satisfied with how today has gone so far.

I drop my gear bag in the foyer with a loud thud after I get home from lunch with Patrick. I've got the rest of the day to myself. I should probably unpack my shit and get settled in a bit more, but fuck that, it'll get done eventually. I head to my bedroom to take a nap, and find that black bra sitting on my bed.

My room still smells like sex.

My dick twitches in interest. Sitting on the edge of the bed, I take the bra in one hand and pull out my phone with the other.

I start searching for Brenna on social media and luckily, she isn't too hard to find - Brenna isn't exactly a common name, and I know she lives in Chicago. Her profile picture is of her and a brunette, obviously friends, laughing together. Her profile says

that she attended Northwestern University and studied
Marketing there.

   With another glance at her bra, I click the "Send Message"
button and start typing.

Hey Brenna,

*Had a great time with you last night. You forgot your bra here. Would you
like to meet up for coffee and I can return it to you?*

Ryan

   I was only wanting a one night stand, but.. she was a lot of
fun. We clicked so well while talking at the bar, plus I don't have
any other friends in Chicago yet. It's worth a try.

   And she's hot as hell. That doesn't hurt anything either.

   After sending the message, I set down my phone and pick
up her bra with one hand, my other hand snaking down the
front of my pants. I've got time to kill.

5. BRENNA

I cried the entire way home in the Uber. The poor driver probably wishes he'd ended his Saturday night one pickup earlier so he didn't have to deal with my sobbing self the entire ride. He probably gave me a one-star rating and I can't say I blame him.

I can't believe I did something so reckless, trashy and stupid. It was insane. It was irresponsible.

It was absolutely incredible.

But it shouldn't have been.

But it was.

I've never experienced pleasure anywhere near that level until last night with Ryan. He must be some kind of sex god, because I am pretty sure it doesn't get any better than an orgasm that completely obliterates you like last night's did.

But it was dirty, foolish and wrong of me to go home with him. I could have been drugged, raped, and left for dead. I was drunk, and feeling bad about myself, so I wasn't thinking straight. I can't believe I let myself get into such a risky situation.

Thankfully, Carly was waiting for me at the front door when the Uber pulled up to our house. John had gone home, luckily - we're all close and he knows a lot about me, but I wasn't exactly ready to have him hear all about my bad decision.

She pulled me inside and over Ben and Jerry's I told her everything that happened. Carly insisted that I go get myself checked out first thing in the morning, but I didn't want to go to the ER since it's a Sunday and my family doctor isn't in until Monday, so I'm going tomorrow instead. If I contracted any STDs, they'll still be there tomorrow, I guess.

Carly was supportive as any best friend should be, but she also took interest in the fact that the sex was good. Well, better than good, but I tried to gloss over the details of just how good it was. I'd rather just forget it ever happened. It was one night. One stupid, amazing night.

So when I'm cleaning around the house and my phone dings with a message from Ryan, I'm stunned. He found my bra, and he sought me out on social media to give it back. And invite me to coffee. He's probably just trying to be nice. He has no other reason to seek me out.

Curiosity overtakes me, and I click his name to go to his profile. His picture is of him standing with a couple other guys, all shirtless and holding a beer, on a large yacht overlooking wide open waters. His smile outshines the other guys by miles and I catch myself smiling along with him before I remember I'm mad at this guy and wipe the smile from my face.

I scroll down into the About Me section of his profile.

Name: Ryan Flynn.

Hometown: Toronto, Canada.

Well, that confirms my suspicion that I was catching snippets of a Canadian accent in his voice last night.

Then I find something I didn't expect.

Occupation: Winger for the Chicago Velocity Hockey Organization.

I don't follow hockey very closely, but I'm a Chicago native and this city loves their hockey, so I know enough about the sport to realize that I fucked a famous athlete last night.

My head spins and I gingerly sit on the edge of my bed to try to quell the sudden onset vertigo. Somehow the gravity of realizing I spread my legs for someone who is probably a well-known hockey star makes me feel even more sick. It probably should make me feel special but instead I want to take the scrubbing brush from the kitchen sink and scrub my vagina with it.

After all, sports stars are usually mansluts. I've heard plenty of rumors about all kinds of famous athletes, since Chicago is home to so many big teams. I never seem to hear any good stories about hockey players settling down, though. Rather, I see the tabloid headlines of scandals and infidelities committed by

Chicago's hockey team and now I'm almost certain I probably have an STD. Or two or three.

I walk into Carly's bedroom, not even bothering to knock. Thankfully, she's sitting on her bed, painting her toenails a neon pink color. She barely has time to screw the cap on her polish before I shove my phone into her hands.

Her brow furrows as she looks at Ryan's profile. "Um..?"

"That's him, Carls."

She scrutinizes the screen for barely half a second before she recognizes the man in the photo. "Ryan Flynn?" she asks, standing up suddenly. Her nail polish goes flying to the floor. "You fucked RYAN FLYNN?"

"Shush!" I'm fairly certain the entire city block just heard Carly yell out my sexual indiscretions.

She grabs my shoulders and shakes me. "Bren! He's in the NHL. He was just traded here from the Drivers. He's kind of a big deal!"

"I have no clue who the Drivers are," I say, prying her hands from my shoulders.

"They're another NHL team, from Philadelphia," Carly says this like its common knowledge. I guess when your fiancé is a big hockey buff, these things become common knowledge for you. "He had a rough season last year, but he's usually a really solid player, so Chicago picked him up on a trade over the summer."

"This isn't helping me feel any better about the situation."

36

Carly pulls me into a hug. "Sorry, Bren. It just isn't very often that your best friend fucks a hockey star. How did you find his profile, anyway? Were you missing him? Oh my God, so if you really fucked Ryan Flynn then he must be super built, huh? I need to know all the details!"

"Carly!" I pull away from her. "Focus! This isn't something to get excited over, remember? And I wasn't missing him. He sought me out. I left my bra at his house and he wants to give it back, apparently."

She twists a lock of her dark hair around her finger, looking thoughtful. "So he looked you up?"

"Yes," I sigh. "I'm trying to forget the whole thing even happened. Why would I go searching for him?"

"I was hoping maybe you weren't regretting it today as much as you were last night?" She offers with a shrug. "I mean, come on Bren - people have one night stands all the time. It's no big deal in this day and age."

Scoffing, I turn to head out of her room. "Maybe not to you, but to me, it's a huge deal."

"Bren, wait," Carly grabs my arm, stopping me in the doorway. "I'm not trying to minimize what happened."

I cross my arms over my chest. "It sure sounds like you are."

Carly shakes her head and sighs. "I'm sorry, Brenna. My goal is to offer another perspective for you and try to help ease your mind a little. You can't go back and undo what you did, and it may not seem like a good thing right now, but who knows? Maybe this will end up being a positive in your life."

"Yeah, okay, sure," I say with a roll of my eyes. I can't imagine ever seeing this as a positive, but I don't feel like being part of this discussion anymore. Carly will keep fighting to prove her side, so it's easier just to give in and move on. This knowledge has seen our friendship through many difficult times.

She claps her hands together between us. "So the real question is - Are you going to respond to him?"

I had forgotten all about how I found Ryan's profile in the first place. "Highly unlikely. Like I said, I'm trying to forget this ever happened."

"I think you should go," Carly says with a devious glint in her eye. "Figure out what this guy's M.O. is. I mean, he cared enough to seek you out on social media. He remembered your name."

I narrow my eyes at her. "You just want me to go out with him because he's a hot, famous hockey player."

Carly shrugs, twisting her hair around her finger again. "You caught me there. But if you were interested enough in this guy - drunk or not - to do naughty things with him.. isn't it at least worth a sober revisit?"

I absently roll my phone over and over in my hand. "You aren't going to let me say no, are you?"

"Nope."

6. BRENNA

Ryan doesn't waste any time. He arranges to meet the very next day for dinner. He explains that he has work for most of the day starting at 6am, hence doing dinner. He doesn't specify what kind of work, but I'm assuming it's something hockey related. I'm trying to convince myself it isn't a date. After all, he's just returning my bra to me.

But somehow, I'm looking forward to this, more than I should.

My doctor appointment in the morning went well. Everything came back clean, thank you sweet baby Jesus. With that weight off my chest, I'm feeling more relaxed - and finding myself interested in Ryan's motives.

I find myself struggling to remain focused the entire day at work. Thankfully, I have a private office and am only bothered once the entire day by my boss, Jackson. I work in the marketing department for an up-and-coming tech company that is headquartered in San Francisco, but has satellite offices in Chicago, New York, and Atlanta. It's a great gig and I'm thankful that I was able to find a job in my field right after graduation, but sometimes I definitely feel out of my league. They took a huge risk with me being inexperienced in the workforce, but I figure as long as I keep giving 110% every day, I'll be a valuable asset to them.

My job mainly consists of small projects that Jackson sends my way. He heads up the department and manages 90% of the workload, somehow. I think he struggles with delegating and ends up overloading himself, but my coworker, Natalie, thinks he just wants to take the credit for everything. Which he sometimes does. But I prefer to think it isn't on purpose.

Thankfully, because Jackson sucks at delegating, I usually only have a small project or two to work on each day. That means that I have the majority of my day at work to do other things. Most of the time I pick up quick and easy freelance jobs on Craigslist, things like logos for photographers or cover art for local bands, and do those. I know it sounds horrible since I'm working for other people while I'm at work, but I'm building my portfolio, and I also need the money.

Finally, 5pm hits and I head out to the restaurant. I specifically picked a place near my workplace so I knew the area well, and also so I didn't have to move my car from my reserved space in the parking garage and try to find a place to park elsewhere. Parking in downtown is crazy stupid unless you pay for a reserved space in a garage. It's an added expense, but it sure beats walking eight blocks in the wintertime.

I also chose the restaurant based on the fact that Ryan asked me to choose a place - probably because he doesn't know Chicago all that well yet. I picked one of my favorite places just up the block from the office and told Ryan to meet me there at 5:15.

I arrive a couple minutes early and take a seat near the door. The patio is open and heavy late summer air floats through the restaurant. I know that soon, fall will officially be here, and I try not to think about the inevitable depression that will overcome me during that time.

My phone buzzes in my purse with a text. I pull it out and laugh when I see that it is Ryan.

The only thing worse than the traffic in Chicago is the parking!

With a giggle, I type back *Welcome to Chi-town!*

It buzzes again, and my smile falls when I see the phone number pop up on the screen. Ashton.

B, I'm sure you were thinking about me, because I never stop thinking about you.

Ugh. I delete the message. He sends me a few texts every once in a while but I never respond to them.

I throw my phone back into my purse as Ryan comes walking in, and my muscles immediately tense with recognition.

41

Recognition of those iceberg colored eyes. Recognition of his stylish brown hair and scruffy face. Recognition of his biceps, tight against a dark blue t-shirt. Recognition of the tattoos covering the entire length of both arms.

He approaches the table, smiling, and holding a large cardboard box. "Hey Brenna!" He slides into the booth and passes the box across the table to me expectantly.

"What is this?"

"What do you think it is?" I can barely see his eyes over the top of the box. I notice that the side of it says 'Kitchen.'

"Plates and silverware? How thoughtful!" I say with a smirk. Sometimes when I'm nervous my brain defaults to sarcasm.

I start to open the box, but Ryan grabs my hand to stop me. It jolts me so hard that I pull away as if I've been burnt. I stare at my hand, bewildered, and somewhere distantly hear Ryan say, "It has the thing in it. You know, what you left at my house. I was trying to be discreet and not just hand it to you in public for everyone to see. But this was one of the only empty boxes I had at my house."

I feel like an idiot and I'm blushing. "Well, thanks Ryan. I appreciate you giving it back to me." I take the box and set it in the booth next to me.

The waitress comes by at this point and takes our drink orders. I get a Coke and Ryan opts for a beer. The waitress, a busty blonde with a ton of eyeshadow on, winks at Ryan as she leaves. I pretend not to notice that, or how she swings her hips as she walks back toward the bar. He doesn't seem to notice her, though. Rather, I'm the recipient of the heat of his stare.

"So.. why did you run off so quickly the other night?"

Apparently Ryan doesn't wait around and just cuts straight to the chase. I nearly choke on my own spit.

"Umm.."

"I'm just curious," he says, his hands up in mock surrender. He leans forward, a devious look on his face. Then he whispers, "Was I that bad?"

He's being cocky and teasing me and yet, behind this front, he seems to genuinely want to know. I decide to play along instead.

"Yeah, you were terrible," I say with an eye roll. "I would give it a 1 out of 10, and that's only because you at least had the required equipment to perform the task."

His eyebrows raise, and I notice a tiny white scar above the left one. "So you noticed my equipment, huh?" His already deep voice is even lower. He leans forward and says just above a whisper, "Was it sufficient for completing the task?"

I feel a blush rising up my neck and I clear my throat. I am sitting in front of the single most beautiful man I have ever seen in my entire life and not only have we had sex, but he looked me up online to give my bra back to me, and now is flirting with me in public while sober. Me. Brenna Wilson. As pathetically average and hopeless as they come.

"Hello? What will you be having?" The busty blonde waitress is standing over me, clearly annoyed and wanting to take my order. I shake my head to clear my thoughts and order my favorite chicken wrap from memory. She snaps her gum before turning to Ryan and attempting to blind him with a sickly sweet smile. He orders a steak without so much as a glance at her, and she lingers a moment too long before wiggling back to the bar.

"Where did you go, Brenna?" Ryan asks, his voice soft, his face etched with concern.

"Nowhere," I stammer. "Sometimes I get lost in my own head. Sorry about that."

"Nothing to be sorry for," he says with a comforting smile. "So tell me about yourself." He crosses his massive, solid arms across his equally massive, solid chest as he leans back in the booth.

I try to swallow back the intimidation and confusion I feel and just stick to answering the questions without humiliating myself. "Not much to tell, really. I'm a native Chicagoan. I do graphic design and marketing work for a company here in Chicago. That's about it."

"That's awful thin on the details," Ryan chuckles. "What about your parents? Any siblings? A husband, kids?" His smile is wide.

"Very funny," I return. "No husband or kids. Not even a boyfriend." I purposely skip the family talk. No way in hell I'm opening Pandora's box with him. After all, after tonight's non-date, I will probably never see nor hear from this guy again. And that's probably for the best.

7. RYAN

I hadn't realized how truly beautiful Brenna is until I'm sitting in front of her. Her hair is in a loose bun, with pieces sticking out in all directions. She is rocking a makeup-free look, not that she needs it. Her white, mostly straight teeth are the highlight of her beautiful smile.

She seems so uncomfortable, though. I know she is shy but it almost feels like it runs deeper than that - like maybe she doesn't understand how beautiful and funny and interesting she is.

We are finally forced to broach the subject of my hockey status when a kid and his dad come up to our table to ask for an autograph. I haven't been recognized a ton in Chicago yet, but I know that soon enough it'll be like it was back in Philadelphia - being stopped on every block for selfies and signatures. It's part of the life and I enjoy meeting the fans. I know simply showing them kindness and giving them a few minutes of my time leaves a lasting impression, and is part of my duty as an athlete. Brenna only seems moderately surprised as I sign a napkin for the kid and pose for a photo with him. Once they leave and I settle back into the booth, she says, "So you really are famous then, huh?"

"I suppose you could say that," I reply, taking a swig of my beer. "I am guessing you looked me up?"

"It was your social media profile, actually." She is playing with the edge of her napkin, running it between her fingers. "Formerly of the Philadelphia Drivers, now traded to the Chicago Velocity."

"Do you follow hockey?" I ask her.

The panic that quickly crosses her face says everything – she has no clue about hockey. "My roommate and her fiancé are big into it. Carly - that's my roommate - knew who you were before I did."

"So you were telling your roommate about me, eh?" I smirk at her, glowing with satisfaction when a flush creeps up into her cheeks.

"Not exactly," she stammers. Luckily for her, our food arrives, and our waitress once again tries way too hard to get my attention. Unfortunately for her, my attention is being held by the beautiful and intriguing woman sitting across the table from me.

After dinner (for which Brenna insisted on paying for her own meal, against my protests to let me take care of it) and conversation, I walk her to her car. She has a reserved spot in a garage just down the block, which is lucky for her because I had to park in some garage several blocks away and that charges something like $20 per hour. I need to remember to ask the guys on the team how they get around in this city.

Brenna's car is a beat-up old silver Beetle. It looks like it has seen better days, but I somehow doubt any of those days took place within this decade. Brenna seems embarrassed over it. I like nice cars, but if it runs, that's cool too. She's seemed embarrassed about a lot of things throughout the course of the evening, though. She's confusing and interesting and cute as hell.

I try not to stare at her glorious ass as she leans across the seat of her car, placing the large cardboard box containing only her black bra onto the passenger seat. She straightens and faces me, brushing her long wavy hair from her eyes. I kind of wish I would have put something else in that box just to screw with her, like a big rock or a kitten or something.

"Thank you for returning my bra to me," she says, holding out her hand to shake mine. I raise an eyebrow at her and her hand visibly falters. She stares back at me, confused, as I take a step closer to her, standing only a few inches away. It's close enough that I can clearly smell her light floral perfume.

The electricity between us is magnified as I lean in closer to her. Those brown eyes stay focused on mine, unwavering, until they finally break and glance down at my mouth. I take that as my cue and lightly brush my lips over hers. She stiffens, and I immediately pull back.

"I-I have to go," she stutters, pulling away as if she's been burned. She immediately gets into her car as I stand there, dumbfounded. She shuts the door and starts the engine at the same time, the Beetle turning over twice before sputtering to life. I step back as she quickly reverses the car out of the space and, without so much as a glance back at me, drives away.

I'm confused and frustrated. It had seemed to me that dinner had gone very well. She was embarrassed and maybe even a bit shy, but I had felt the sizzling connection between us. I know I did.

I'm used to getting what I want. And right now, I want that girl in my bed again.

The next morning at practice, I grab my phone during a water break and navigate to Brenna's profile again. I haven't gone so far as to send her a friend request yet, but I've been looking at her profile to try to learn more about her. She doesn't have a lot on there. Most of her photos are of her and another girl who is tagged as Carly who I remember she mentioned is her roommate. It seems like Brenna and Carly are close friends, along with Carly's fiancé John.

I am able to get the name of Brenna's work from her profile, and decide to reach out to her to see if I can fix whatever in the world happened at the end of our date last night. A quick call to the first florist that popped up in a google search has a big bouquet being sent to Brenna's office along with a note. I had them simply write "To: Brenna, From: Ryan" on it. It doesn't feel incredibly forward and since I have no idea why she completely wigged out, it's worth a try.

A message is waiting on my phone when I head to my locker after practice.

Why did I receive flowers from you?

I type back, *Does a guy need a reason to be sweet? Besides, you wouldn't let me buy your dinner last night, so I figured you couldn't say no to flowers.*

She quickly responds, *Sorry, I don't usually get gifts from guys. Or have them pay for my meals. This is a little out of the ordinary for me.*

I hop in the locker room shower and mull over her message. Usually girls love receiving gifts and having a guy be chivalrous - but something makes me think that it isn't that she's being ungrateful but rather just that she hasn't been doted on before.

Something about Brenna interests me. She isn't a bunny, for one. She seems smart and creative. She's also sexy as hell. But she's intriguing to me, and the fact that she's ran away from me twice now only fuels my desire to catch her.

As a rule, I don't pursue the same girl twice. Once I either get turned down or get her in the sack, then we're done. Usually I get bored once I've sealed the deal.

But I'm not bored of Brenna yet and I can't figure out why.

I towel off and throw on my clothes before messaging her back, *I'm sorry. I hope it doesn't seem weird or forward. I think you're cool and I'd like to keep getting to know you.*

I hit send on the message before I have time to puss out and throw my phone in my bag. I sling it over my shoulder and say bye to Matus, one of our defenseman from Slovakia, and Nils, a center from Sweden.

One of the assistant coaches stops me on my way out of the locker room. "Flynn, do you have a sec?"

"Sure, what's up?" I say, leaning against the cinder block wall behind me.

"Real impressive playing out there so far," he says warmly. "I know you had a rough year last year, but I think you're going to do great things for this team."

"Thanks, Coach. I appreciate the faith in me, and the opportunity to play here in Chicago."

He pats me on the arm and heads down one of the side hallways leading to the offices. My smile is big when I leave the building, but it's even bigger when I check my phone again later and find a message from Brenna, asking to meet me for coffee.

8. BRENNA

I already couldn't stop thinking about Ryan, but when the bouquet showed up at my office door? My stomach did little summersaults at the sight of it.

It means he's thinking about me, too.

Ashton had NEVER bought me gifts, even when we were "together." He also never paid for my meals. So to have a seriously hot hockey player wanting to buy me flowers, take me to dinner, and just be around me in general? I must be dreaming.

Natalie immediately comes into my office after the administrative assistant stops off the flowers, kicking my door shut behind her. "What a gorgeous bouquet! Who is it from?"

"Oh, uh, he's just a friend. I think." Wow, way to go, Brenna.

Natalie squeals in delight as she perches on the edge of my desk. She sniffs one of the flowers. "Looks like he wants to be more than friends to me!" She winks at me. "You get 'em, Tiger."

I laugh, flushed with embarrassment. "Natalie, you're acting like this is the 8th grade and I just got my first boyfriend."

"Psh, Brenna. I know these aren't from what's-his-ass so this practically IS your first boyfriend!" Natalie, like everyone else in my life, hates Ashton with a fiery passion. "What's-his-ass doesn't count, obviously."

"Well, thanks, Natalie. I don't know if I'd call him my boyfriend yet though. Things are a little confusing right now."

Natalie leans in closer to me. "How so?"

I give her a brief rundown of what happened yesterday, completely skipping over our initial meeting. I like Natalie well enough, but we aren't that close, and she can be quite the gossip.

"I like this guy already, Brenna," she says, hopping off my desk and heading for the door. "Keep him close. And keep me updated."

Eventually, I decide to ask to meet with Ryan for coffee. We need to figure out where this may or may not be going, before I get my heart involved.

Ryan is waiting for me at the coffee shop I chose partway between work and my house. His shoulders are nearly bursting out of his shirt. I feel my stomach do another flip as his eyes meet mine and an easy smile graces his scruffy face. "Hi Brenna."

"Hi Ryan," I say shyly as I sit down across from him. The tables here must have been made for people under 5 feet tall, so Ryan looks like a giant here.

"I would have gotten you a drink, but I don't know what you like." He stands up from the table. "What would you like?"

"You don't have to get it for me," I say quickly, starting to stand.

Ryan's hand on mine stops me in my tracks. "Please, I would like to get you a drink. What would you like?"

I sink back into my seat. "A small hot chocolate, please." He smiles at me and turns to head for the counter. It presents me the perfect opportunity to admire all 6'2" of muscle and sex appeal.

The man is built like a god. He could probably lift a car by himself and not break a sweat. I didn't realize I was so interested in arms and shoulders but I certainly am now. And that ass! It must have been custom-built by the Lord himself.

I snap back to my senses when Ryan sits down across from me, and hands me my hot chocolate with a smirk. "See something you like, Brenna?" He breaks into a grin when I blush. I hide behind my cup, sipping gingerly on my hot chocolate as my embarrassment subsides.

"So I think we should talk about last night," Ryan leads off. I cross my legs and run my finger around the edge of my cup. "Did I read the signs wrong?" he asks gently.

I run my finger around the cup a few more times, biting my lip. "No, you didn't. But... what are we doing here, Ryan? What is this? Because what I thought was a one-night-stand has suddenly become dinner, flowers, and now coffee."

"You're the one who suggested coffee," he teases me. "And I thought it was just one night too." He leans back, pausing, one hand stroking his bearded chin. "But the next morning, I was still thinking about you. And then yesterday at dinner, I had such a great time with you... I want to keep getting to know you."

My head is spinning. "I-I'm nothing special."

"Why in the world would you think that?"

My palms are sweaty and I feel the panic bubbling up in my chest, along with the familiar, overwhelming feeling of never being good enough. I can't control what comes bursting out of me. "Because you're a hockey-playing Canadian demigod and I'm just... me."

Ryan is silent, staring me down, his expression unreadable. We are both frozen, eyes locked with each other. After several moments, he suddenly stands up, grabbing my hand and urging me up with him. I barely have time to grab my purse before he's pulling me out the door of the coffee shop into a back alley.

His large hands grab my shoulders and gently - but with fervor - push me up against the brick wall. Shallow breaths escape my lips and all I hear is a low hum in my head. I can see nothing but this man, standing in front of me, his hand cupping my cheek.

Ryan slowly brings his face within inches of mine, closing the distance between us. After an agonizing moment of tension and terror, his mouth seals over mine.

All at once, my body is ablaze. Every sense kicks into overdrive as our tongues intertwine. A moan escapes me and it seems to kick Ryan up a notch as he sucks on my bottom lip.

My mind is on fire. Why do I have such a connection with this guy? Why do we keep ending up like this? And why am I constantly grasping at the very edges of my good judgment when I'm around him?

It was supposed to be just one night, but my resolve is disappearing with every moment I spend with him. With every kiss he plants on my lips, I am pulled in deeper by this man.

We break apart after a few hot and heavy minutes, both panting heavily, and his intense crystalline eyes are locked with mine. "You're amazing, Brenna. Please... stop running from this."

9. RYAN

We barely make it through the front door of my house before my shirt comes off. I kick the door shut with my foot and help Brenna out of her shirt, which is stuck on her ponytail. Her milky skin is smooth, with lean muscle and gentle curves on a delicate frame. I take a moment to appreciate the beautiful woman standing in front of me.

But only a moment.

I seal my mouth over hers, my hands reaching for her ass, pulling her off her feet and her pelvis up to mine. She wraps her legs around my torso and grinds against me, causing me to involuntarily groan into her mouth. Still kissing her, I hold the back of her head with one hand and unclasp her bra with the other, discarding the garment without any grace. That's probably how her last one ended up being left here, but I'm too horny to care. I palm her breast with one hand, the other cupping her ass to support her weight as we grind against each other.

I don't know what it is about this woman, but she drives me crazy in the best way.

She's kissing my neck, her sweet little mouth hot against my skin. My dick is wedged in-between us, begging to be freed. I finally grunt out "Too many clothes." She pauses, nodding, and we disconnect long enough to hastily shove our pants and underwear down our legs. I settle for mine staying pooled at my ankles. I take a second and grab the condom I keep in my wallet and toss it on the table next to us.

I pull Brenna against me and hook her legs around my body again before swinging us both around, roughly pinning her against the foyer wall. Her eyes are full of fire, her blonde hair flowing across her soft, delectable skin.

The first (and last) time I had her naked, we were both a little too intoxicated to fully enjoy each other. But I can tell that this time, it's as if she's seeing me for the first time. Her eyes have been roaming my body appreciatively, her hands running up and down my arms. Knowing she's enjoying what she sees is only serving to ramp me up even more.

I take one of her perky, pink nipples into my mouth and lightly tug on it with my lips, smiling against her breast when she moans in response. She threads her hands in my hair, her elbows on my shoulders, supporting her weight in addition to her strong thighs wrapped around me. She's hot and damp against me, grinding herself against my length, and I'm having to restrain myself from just going crazy on her.

I can't hold back much longer, though. The need to be balls deep inside Brenna overwhelms me, and I fumble my hand across the table until I find the familiar foil. I pull her a little higher up on me and roll the condom on underneath her.

"You doing okay?" I ask her.

"Never better," she says breathily, her eyelids heavy. "Just glad I haven't skipped yoga class lately."

I laugh as I navigate my dick to her entrance, feeling how slick she is. I could swear that I feel her whimper under my touch. Gently, I guide myself in, exhaling slowly as she slides down onto me, taking my full length inside herself.

She shifts her weight on me and I groan into her neck, breathing in the sweet scent of her skin. My hands on her ass, I urge her up and down my cock, pulling back on each retreat and thrusting into her a little harder each time.

I watch her supple breasts shake with each thrust. Listening to the pitch of her moans rising higher and higher, I amp up the vigor of my thrusts, while urging myself to hang on a little longer.

I pull her arms from around my neck and, grabbing her hands, pin them to the wall above her head. The sound that escapes her is feral. It only serves to push me harder into her.

It isn't long before her moans turn into screams and I watch as the orgasm rips through her, shredding her before my very eyes. A couple frantic thrusts later and I'm chasing her over the edge, pumping every last bit of myself into her.

Every part of my body is numb with pleasure. We're both panting, her breath tickling my sweat-slicked skin. She leans her head back against the wall behind her, eyes closed, orgasmic bliss in her smile. After a minute, she dismounts me and I quickly dispose of the condom. Our clothes are a haphazard mess all across the foyer floor. I don't even care.

"Shower?" I ask her.

An hour and two more orgasms later, Brenna is tucked up against me under the sheets, her wet hair splayed across the pillow. I trail my hand lazily across her arm, back and forth and in slow, deliberate circles. I don't cuddle puck bunnies, but I don't feel awkward cuddling like this with her.

Everything feels peaceful and comfortable with Brenna, like we've known each other for much longer than just a couple of days.

"Ryan?" her voice is soft, almost dream-like.

"Yes?"

"We haven't eaten yet." As if on cue, my stomach rumbles.

"Shit," I say. "I can order a pizza. Is that cool?"

"Yes, please."

I sit up against the pillow, grabbing my phone off the nightstand and a few clicks later, and a pizza is ordered and on it's way. I toss my phone onto the nightstand and wrap my arm back around her.

"Tell me more about your job," I say to her. "What do you do, exactly?"

She shifts a bit so she can look at me while she talks. I can see the passion in her eyes before she even begins to speak. "I work in the marketing department for a bio-tech company. Mostly, we focus on ways to use technology to make daily life easier for people who deal with a lot of different conditions – diabetes, insomnia, and seizures, to name a few. We make a lot of smartphone apps, but we are also starting to dabble in wearables like smartwatches."

"As in apps for the smartwatches?" I ask.

"Apps, or even designing our own wearables," she says. "We're a small company, so that sort of thing is still a long ways away."

I roll onto my side so I can face her. "So what do you do for the marketing side of things?"

"My department is responsible for letting the target audience know about our products and projects. My boss, Jackson, handles most of the big stuff, but he delegates a lot of the graphic design stuff to me. Brochures, website and social media graphics, that sort of thing."

She's clearly passionate about what she does. "That's really neat that you're involved in something that can help so many people."

"Yeah, it's really rewarding to see and hear how our products have helped someone," she says, smiling. "I enjoy it a lot."

"Did you go to school for graphic design?" I ask her. I already know the answer from her social media profile, but I'd rather ask her directly so I don't feel so stalker-ish about it.

"I did. I went to Northwestern. It's where I met my roommate, Carly."

I reflect back to the photos I saw on her profile and picture a brunette girl in my mind. "She's the girl who just got engaged, right?"

Brenna's face flashes dark for just a moment. I would have missed it if I hadn't been looking right at her. "Yes," is her simple reply.

I want to question her reaction, but I'm stopped by the sound of the doorbell signaling the arrival of pizza. I swing my legs out of bed, slip on my boxers and a pair of athletic shorts, and head to the front door.

Brenna and I lay in bed for several hours, cuddling and talking, getting to know each other. I learn that her favorite food is chicken nuggets, she enjoys listening to disco music, and that she's always wanted to go to Cabo but has never had the chance.

I've also learned that her coffee-colored eyes make my heart pound. Her smile lights up the entire room. Her passion for many things in life is inspiring.

But I've also learned that she doesn't talk about her family – at all. And her reaction when I mentioned Carly's engagement was confusing at best.

Brenna interests me in a way I haven't been interested in a girl before. Puck bunnies are all vapid, conceited bitches who only care about themselves and getting in bed with hockey players. Brenna isn't like that. She's a breath of fresh air in my stifling world.

10. BRENNA

Ryan offers to take me to work the next morning. He drives me home quickly to change so I don't show up to work in yesterday's clothes. Carly had already left for work at the hospital before I stopped by the house so I let Ryan follow me in, but I make him wait in the living room.

Thankfully I had texted Carly late last night to let her know where I was so she wouldn't worry, and she had set a clean outfit out on my bed for me, along with a note that says "You go, girl!" I roll my eyes as I throw it away.

Dressed and freshened up, I emerge from my room and walk into the living room. Ryan looks like a giant on our tiny, beat up sofa that Carly picked up from a thrift store for fifty bucks last year. I'm suddenly aware of how dingy, run-down and sad our little house feels, especially in comparison to Ryan's beautiful, posh home. I hurry him out the door, embarrassment washing over me.

He takes me through the drive thru of the coffee place near my house and, at his insistence, I order a coffee and a bagel. All too soon, we pull up in front of my office building. It feels strange, getting out of his flashy but classy black Audi, breakfast in hand, on time for work. Normally I'm running into the building ten minutes late in a wrinkled outfit and I'm lucky if I even remembered to grab a snack from the fridge that morning.

"Have a great day at work, Brenna," he smiles at me. "Change some lives today."

My stomach flip flops and my heart threatens to jump out of my chest. I squeak out a "thanks" and shut the car door, hustling for the doorway of the building.

When I reach the door, I turn back and watch him pull away, merging into the stream of morning traffic, and remind myself to breathe.

Ryan mentioned to me last night that he more than likely won't be able to see me again for a couple days because his father will be in town. He didn't elaborate and I didn't pressure him to, but it seemed like he wasn't thrilled about it.

I completely understand, because if my father ever dared to show his face here, I'd be livid.

Last night feels like a dream – the most wonderful, insane, beautiful, stunning dream. Every moment with Ryan feels like magic. He asked so many questions about me – my likes and dislikes, my passions, my dreams.

It's unnerving, because this was only supposed to be one night, but I can easily see it becoming something more.

I'm still trying to keep my distance though. I have to protect my heart because he's still Ryan Flynn, Famous Hockey Player and I'm still Brenna Wilson, Plain and Ordinary Nobody.

I made the mistake of looking him up online immediately after getting to work. Photo after photo of him popped up, some of them with various beautiful women. A little clicking led me to discover the term "puck bunny," which is women who whore themselves out to hockey players. Apparently, there are a lot of them, and they are insanely gorgeous. And insanely slutty.

Of course, in my mind, I know he isn't innocent. But reading these women talk about how they allegedly fucked him back in Philly and even a few back in his hometown of Toronto has my mind spinning.

I can't get my hopes up and I need to stay as detached from him as possible. Famous, gorgeous guys like him don't keep plain girls like me around for long. He's new in town. He will meet new women, get bored with me, move on, and my life will go back to the way it was before he showed up and rocked my world.

Carly meets me for lunch at a cafe near my work that we like to frequent. She works in the Human Resources department at the hospital near my office. She has rigid work hours, and my job is a bit more flexible unless I have a deadline or a conference call. She is already sitting at the table with our food when I arrive.

"Okay Bren – spill! What is happening with you and Ryan?"

"Shush!" I put my hand over her mouth, quieting her like she's a naughty child. "I'll tell you everything, but I need you to bring it down a couple notches."

"Okay, okay, I will try to keep calm," she says with a grin. "This is a big deal though. You stayed the night with him. You haven't even slept with anyone since Fuckface. And I thought this was just a one night stand?"

"Shhhhh!" An older couple a few tables away from us is staring. "Thank you for loudly announcing to the entire restaurant that I got laid last night."

Carly laughs, running a hand absently through her long, dark hair. "I'm sorry, Bren. I'm just so excited for you! My baby girl is getting back out there, and boinking one of the hottest players in the entire NHL."

"Oh my god, Carly. Nobody calls it 'boinking.'" I roll my eyes at her.

"Whatever," she says, tossing a potato chip in her mouth. "So how was it? It must have been good if you stayed the night."

I twist a lock of my hair around my finger, thinking back on last night's multiple orgasms... and the bonus one this

67

morning, too. The sex was absolutely phenomenal – mind-blowing, in fact. "Yeah, it was pretty great," I admit, blushing. It's by far the best I've ever had, but I'm not ready to tell Carly that.

Carly squeals and the couple stares at us again. She shoots them a dirty look, as if they are the ones disturbing her and not the other way around. "So what does this mean? Are you dating?"

"I don't think so," I say, staring at a painting of Lake Michigan hanging on the wall. "He just moved here and doesn't know anyone yet. I'm sure that he sees me as easy tail right now, and as soon as he gets settled, he'll lose my number."

"Oh come on, Bren, you're selling yourself short!" Carly grabs my cheeks and pinches them both. "You're a catch, girl! Any guy would be the luckiest guy on earth to have you as their girlfriend!"

I bat Carly's hands away, laughing. "Okay, okay, Miss Motivation. I'm still not getting my hopes up. Besides, he said he won't be able to see me for a couple days because his father will be in town, so we'll see if he calls me this weekend or not. If he does, cool. If not, then we never talk about him or this two-night-stand ever again. Okay?"

"If you insist," Carly replies, stuffing a chip in her mouth. "I'm calling it now though – you're going to fall in love with that man."

I throw one of my chips at her, hopeful and terrified that she might be right.

"So have you started looking for a new roommate yet?" Carly asks out of nowhere.

I choke on a piece of bread and chug some of my water to push it down. "Uh, not yet."

"Bren! You need to start looking, and soon! The wedding is only a few months away!"

I nod in agreement and hastily change the subject. It feels like I've barely seen Carly since I met Ryan, and I know I'll have to get used to seeing her less. Soon she'll be married and living with John and I'll be… up a creek, unable to afford to live on my own.

But I can't think about those things right now. It'll all work itself out in the end.

I hope.

11. RYAN

I practiced hard today. I should have been worn out after last night with Brenna, but knowing that when I got home my father would be there fueled my aggression, and I channeled it into my drills.

My judgmental, freeloading, waste of space creator decided he wanted to stop by for a couple days to "wish me luck" with my new team.

More like he wanted to come and fuck with my head.

My father wanted my brother Sam, who was four years older than me, to be a big-time hockey star. Sam was perfect both on and off the ice, but he was a rink rat through and through. The scouts were all over him from a young age, and everyone knew Sam would do big things in hockey. I played too, but Sam was truly a star and destined for greatness.

I loved and admired everything about my older brother. He was my confidante, my hero, and my best friend.

But at sixteen years old, while drinking with friends and skating on our private lake way too late into the springtime, Sam fell through the ice.

He drowned, and our lives were turned upside-down.

My mom immediately checked out. Overnight, she went from trophy housewife to a silent stranger occupying our house, drifting through each day with vacant eyes.

My father, on the other hand, became angry. Aggressive. Violent. Sam's body wasn't even in the ground before my father began to increase my practices. First it was just the frequency. He said I needed to get into better shape because, heading into puberty, I wasn't as lean as Sam had been.

Then the practices began to increase in brutality. I would be woken up at three in the morning and dragged outside in my pajamas in all seasons to work on my slapshot against the garage door. There were days he would force me to skate around the lake for hours straight without a break. Eventually, he took to shooting a paintball gun at me if I slowed down. He would sit on the end of the dock, a beer in one hand and paintball gun in the other, watching me with an ever-present scowl.

I couldn't be drafted soon enough.

Going to Philly and getting away from the hell I'd been trapped in for six years was such a relief. I hadn't realized how miserable I was until I was away from it all.

71

I felt awful for leaving my mom behind with that terrible man, but unfortunately, I couldn't save us both.

Now, my father shows up roughly once per year at my door. He uses the opportunity to tell me what I'm door wrong in my life and what I need to work on in my game, because even after getting drafted into the NHL at eighteen, I still wasn't good enough for him.

I wasn't on the first line.

I wasn't one of the top three stars of each game.

I wasn't on every highlight reel.

I wasn't Sam.

As expected, when I walk into my house, I can already tell he's here. It isn't an obvious sign, but rather the sense of foreboding that encompasses me the moment I step over the threshold. I toss my bag down on the floor of the foyer and head into the kitchen, where I find him sitting at the island with three bottles of beer next to him. His beard is unkempt and his clothes are wrinkled and dirty. When he sees me, his blue eyes are dark.

"Son," he addresses me simply.

"Sir," I return, curtly, as I pull two bottles of water from the fridge. I set one in front of him even though I know it won't be touched.

He takes a swig from his beer bottle and says, "Nice place you got here. A little small though. Couldn't you have gotten something bigger with your new salary, even after the pay cut?"

Anger flashes white-hot through me, but I quickly push it down. "This is just a rental. I'm going to buy something later in the season."

He grunts in response and takes another pull from the bottle. I walk into the living room and flop down on the couch, turning on ESPN. I have to remind myself that he will only be here for a couple of days, and then he'll be out of my life again for another year or so. I can get through a few days of misery.

I could always tell him no, that he can't visit me, but my conscience won't allow me to do that. I keep hoping that one of these times, he'll come around and be the amazing dad he used to be. That maybe he'll admit that he tried to turn me into his dead son and he'll apologize for it all.

I know it won't happen, yet I still hope for it.

"It's a shame you couldn't have gotten traded to a real good team like Detroit or Toronto," I hear from behind me. His thick accent is slurred with the booze. "Real fine teams, those are. Of course, you were on a real fine team, but look what happened there. Shame, real shame."

Just a couple days, Flynn, I tell myself. *Just a couple days.*

12. BRENNA

Friday rolls around, and I haven't heard from Ryan since Tuesday, the morning he dropped me off at work. I try not to let it bother me, but I find myself checking my phone for messages from him way more than I should be. Natalie stops by my office even more than usual, asking about my "mystery boyfriend" and it only makes me more anxious to hear from him.

But I won't chase him. I won't text him first. He said I wouldn't hear from him for a few days, so I do my best to give him space, even though it's eating me alive.

I spent the better part of eight years chasing Ashton and what did that get me? Nothing but disappointment and bitter heartbreak. It's best for all involved for me to not chase after Ryan.

As I'm about to leave the office on Friday for a much-needed weekend, my phone dings with an incoming message. My heart skips a beat as Ryan's name finally flashes across the screen.

My father is gone. I need to see you. Can you come over?

Pulling my office door shut and locking it, I lean back against it and type out *Yes, but is it cool if I stop at my place to grab a few things first?*

Ryan quickly sends back *Okay.* I hurry to the parking garage, amazed by how hot it is outside for being the end of September. Soon enough, the air will cool and the Windy City will plunge into another winter. I hate winter and I would much rather it be summer weather all the time.

But maybe now that I'm kind-of involved with a hockey player, winter won't be so bad.

I get to my house in record time. I find Carly and John curled up together in the living room, watching Orange is the New Black on Netflix. "Are you guys seriously watching without me again?" I sigh as I kick the front door shut behind me.

"We're only two episodes ahead of you," Carly says, not taking her eyes off the screen.

"You suck," I whine. They know I'm only kind-of annoyed that they're watching without me. I head into my bedroom, grab my duffel bag, and toss some clothes in it. I also grab my laptop from atop my dresser and put it in my bag as well. I have a few commission pieces I need to do this weekend, and I don't know how long I'll be at Ryan's, so I decide it's better to be safe than sorry.

I'm in the bathroom putting my toothbrush in the bag when Carly comes in and squeals. Thankfully I'm used to her loud squeals and had braced myself for it. "Did he finally message you?"

"Yes, he did," I say with a small smile, grabbing my shampoo and conditioner bottles out of the shower.

"I knew he would!" she says, dancing around the bathroom. "Did you pack something sexy to wear? You aren't taking your retainer, are you? Did you shave?"

"Carly, give her a chance to breathe," John says from the doorway. He leans against the doorframe, chuckling. "What are you two going on about in here?"

"Ryan finally texted Bren," Carly gushes. She wraps her arms around John's waist. "I'm just so excited for her!"

John looks confused. He cocks his head at me. "Is this one-night-stand guy?"

"Two-night-stand, about to be three!" Carly says before I can get any words out. "And he's Ryan Flynn. THE Ryan Flynn."

"The winger from Philly who just got traded here?" John asks Carly. She nods so vigorously that John is shifted off-balance and has to change his stance against the doorframe. "Wow, Brenna. Good for you."

76

"Thanks, I think," I say with a laugh, tossing my hairbrush in the bag. "It's just casual at this point, so nothing to write home about."

"Whatever, Bren," Carly croons. "You and Ryan are going to fall in love and have a super glamorous life together."

"You keep saying that and yet I somehow am not listening to you," I say as I sling the bag over my shoulder and slide around them. "I'm leaving now before you start coming up with names for future children."

"So you're saying there's a chance?" Carly calls after me. The three of us laughing follows me out the front door.

I park in Ryan's driveway and walk up the path to his door. I stop on the porch, staring up at his gorgeous house in this perfect, peaceful neighborhood. My stomach is doing insane flips. What if he wanted to see me to tell me in person that we're done? He's so kind that I could see him being the type of guy to break it to a girl in person rather than through text or something douchey like that.

Gritting my teeth, I ring the doorbell. A few moments later, he appears at the door, in all his gloriousness. It's amazing how in a matter of only three days I had forgotten how absolutely stunning he is. His hair seems shaggier than I remember, his tattoos brighter against his skin than I recall, his legs longer than my memory serves.

His face gives away no emotion, but his eyes are ablaze. "Come in," he says, everything about him rigid. I cautiously walk into the house and take off my shoes in the foyer. Ryan disappears into the bedroom, and I hesitantly follow, confused and with no idea what to expect.

He takes my duffel bag from me and tosses it on the floor of his room. The late-day sun is streaming through his windows, and he pulls the curtains shut. He turns to me, still expressionless.

"Are... are you okay?" I ask, taking a step toward him. He's tense. He keeps flexing and loosening one hand, as if he's trying not to punch something. Or someone. "Ryan?"

"No, I'm not okay," he says. "I need to be inside you. Right now."

"Oh," I squeak out. "Umm.."

He tears his shirt over his head and I'm bombarded by those insane washboard abs and broad shoulders. His shorts and boxers are gone in one swoop and his huge cock is already at full attention.

I haven't moved yet because I'm in shock, so he closes the distance between us and grabs at the hem of my shirt, urging it over my head. It falls to the floor and his hands move to my bra, quickly peeling it from my body. In a daze, I tug down my shorts and panties and step out of them so I am completely naked, standing in front of him.

Ryan grabs my face between his large hands. "I need to apologize to you right now. The last three days have been absolute hell. I need to fuck you so badly, but it's going to be rough."

This doesn't sound like the same Ryan I cuddled with only three short days ago. He sounds detached... almost like he's dead inside. I don't know what transpired over the last three days, but he's hurting, and I hurt for him.

I put my hands over his, running my thumbs across his skin. "That's okay. Whatever you need, I'm here for you."

He kisses the top of my head, lightly, and for a moment, the Ryan from earlier in the week peeks through.

Then, in an instant, I'm being hauled to the bed, and he's climbing on top of me. His lips meet mine and they're at a fever pitch. His hands are already on my breasts, tugging and rolling my nipples between his nimble fingers. He takes one of my nipples into his mouth and a strangled moan escapes me as he sucks and nibbles.

His hand trails it's way down my side, caressing my hip and gripping my thigh. His other hand slides down the length of my body, stopping near the prize to tickle around my entrance, causing my hips to buck. He slips a digit inside, then another, and presses the pad of his thumb against my clit. I feel like I'm on fire. Every nerve in my body is in overdrive as he rubs slow circles with his thumb, caressing me in the deepest way. He works me like that for a few moments, pulling me close to the brink in such a short amount of time.

I shudder when he withdraws from me, but his cock is soon sheathed in latex and pressed against my opening. We lock eyes for a moment. His eyes are stormy and tortured, full of demons. Maybe I should be afraid, but I'm not. I've worn that same look myself, many, many times before. With my permission granted, he presses in and groans as I take him in to the hilt.

He pulls my legs up, my hips lifting off the bed, and wraps them around his waist. Then he leans forward, gripping the top of the headboard with both hands for leverage, and begins moving in and out of me. He hits me deep and I don't hold back my moans. The pace quickly reaches pounding as he slams in and out of me, fucking me harder and faster than I've ever been fucked before.

"Need you with me," he grunts in between thrusts.

"I'm with you," I moan back.

He falls over the edge, shattering into a million pieces before me. His face twists into a mixture of pleasure and despair as he comes. I immediately follow him into orgasm, the force rocketing through me, scorching my entire body from the inside. I rock against him, milking every last wave of pleasure out of the both of us.

Ryan collapses on top of me, and at first I think he's still shuddering from the orgasm, until I realize he's actually crying. I throw my arms around him, holding him as his shoulders heave and he sobs into my neck.

To say I'm stunned would be an understatement. What in the fucking hell happened to Ryan this week?

13. RYAN

My father is the biggest piece of shit I've ever had the displeasure of knowing. I knew that him coming to visit was going to be rough since I was traded due to my slipping performance, but I didn't expect for him to be nearly as shitty and cruel as he was.

I'm twenty-six years old. He shouldn't have this much control over me at this point in my life. I'm a hockey star who has a house and several nice cars and as long as I'm good with my money, I'll be set for life. But every time he blows into town, I'm twelve years old and skating laps around the lake at breakneck speeds again, hoping with every pass around that he won't shoot the paintball gun at me because I'll finally be good enough for him.

I was never good enough then. And I'm still not good enough now.

The entire three days he was here were filled with condescension and judgment. Every move I made was scrutinized. I spent as much time as possible at the private team gym after regular practices so I didn't have to go home and face my father. Even when I finally did come home, he would criticize my workout routine, saying I was working out too much and was going to burn out my shoulders and that's probably why my performance last season was subpar. Those are all his words, not mine. Then he'd criticize my diet, even though I started back on the plan that was customized for me by my personal trainer two weeks ago (minus the pizza I shared with Brenna the other night). All the while, he was bumming on my couch, drinking the entire two-four of beer I had (what Americans call a twenty-four pack) and going through my shit, like always.

Yet I didn't have the heart to kick him out. I can't completely cut him out of my life... because at the end of the day, he's still my father. Unfortunately, he's the only family I have left.

The minute he walked out my door to catch his plane back to Toronto, I texted Brenna. I had forced myself not to think about her for the last three days, because I didn't want to give my father anything more that he could use against me.

But the moment he was gone, she invaded my thoughts. I was so pent up and I needed some kind of release, and I'm so glad she was willing to come over tonight so I could sink myself into her.

I wasn't expecting to break down right after climaxing, though.

Brenna holds me in her arms, grounding me. Using the deep breathing techniques I've been taught by various trainers over the years, I regain my composure. The techniques help keep your anger in check during a game, but I also use them occasionally in off-the-ice situations.

I go to roll off of Brenna, but I'm still inside her, although my dick is now mostly limp. I carefully pull out of her and swing my legs off the side of the bed to dispose of the condom in the can next to my nightstand. She hasn't said anything yet, but I can feel in the air that she's wondering why I called her here just to fuck her and then cry.

"I know I owe you some kind of explanation," I say, still sitting with my back to her. "But I'm not really sure where to start."

I feel her arms wrap around me from behind. "You don't owe me anything, Ryan." She presses her face into my back. "If you want to talk about it, then of course I'll be here to listen, but all I need is to make sure you're okay."

"I'll be okay," I tell her, placing my hands over her arms. I'm already starting to feel much better than I did a few hours ago. It's amazing that something as simple as her presence – her touch – can bring me so much comfort and peace. "Brenna?"

"What?"

"Let's do something fun tonight."

She unwinds herself and sits up behind me. I turn to look at her and find her staring at me like I've grown another head. I clear my throat and try to reign in my thoughts. "I need to get out of the house and get my mind off of things."

She runs her hands over my shoulders. She's still pretty tense, and undoubtedly my sudden 180 has given her whiplash. To her credit, she tries to roll with my out-of-nowhere mood swing. "Um, sure. What did you have in mind?"

"I don't have a plan. I was hoping you'd come up with something."

Brenna slides to the edge of the bed next to me and watches me, a bemused smirk on her beautiful face. "Seriously? You want to do something but you have nothing in mind?"

"Well, you know this area better than I do..." I trail off, standing from the bed and picking up my clothes from the floor.

She's grinning. "You aren't going to be able to use that excuse for forever, you know."

I laugh as I pull on a fresh pair of boxer-briefs. "Yeah, yeah, I know. So what's the plan for tonight?"

"You're seriously making me decide?" she glares at me playfully from the bed where she's sitting, still completely naked.

I toss her shirt at her. "I'm going to pick something random and silly just to spite you," she says.

"Go for it," I reply, leaning down and kissing her softly.

"I'm pretty sure the last time I played mini-putt, I was like, eight," I say.

Brenna flips her hair over her shoulder, squinting her eyes at me. "You told me to pick something to do, and I told you that I was going to choose something random. So here you go." She sticks her tongue out at me, and I stick my tongue out back at her before we both burst into laughter.

The teenage kid at the ticket counter looks like he'd rather be anywhere else on a Friday night. I can't say I blame him. "Two, please," I tell him, pulling out my wallet and handing him the money. He hands Brenna and I each a neon-colored golf ball and a freakishly tiny golf club.

I follow Brenna across the lot to Hole #1. She changed into a pair of tiny denim shorts and a light blue tank top before we left the house. I noticed she had packed a few different outfits, along with toiletries, in her duffel bag. Normally that would piss me off, because girls don't get to stay with me for that long – but I keep reminding myself that Brenna isn't a puck bunny.

"So since you're a pro hockey player, you should be a natural at mini-putt," Brenna says, grinning at me. "However, what you don't realize is that I totally kick ass at mini-putt."

"Oh really?" I smirk at her. "We'll see who is kicking who's ass by the end of this."

Brenna lines up her shot toward a giant plaster elephant with a tunnel for the ball between its feet. She carefully knocks the ball and it rolls through the tunnel and into the hole on the other side.

"Hole in one, baby! That's right!" she cheers for herself, doing a victory dance in the middle of the green. I cross my arms over my chest, playing angry.

"My turn." I set the bright blue ball down on the fake grass and turn to line up my shot. The putter feels like a toy in my hands. I have to bend way down to even get it to reach the ground. "This feels ridiculous. Are the putters always so small?"

"Yes. And you look ridiculous." Brenna has her phone out and snaps a pic of me. I hit the ball, a bit too hard and to the left, and miss the hole by a mile. She laughs, showing me the photo she took of me all hunched over with the putter in hand, and it looks absolutely absurd for someone who is 6'2" to be bent over that far to putt.

I easily sink the ball on the second try and we traipse over to Hole #2. I stare at Brenna's legs while she putts. By Hole #6, she's thoroughly kicking my ass. Golf balls just don't move the same as a hockey puck - at least, that's the excuse I'm going with.

Catching her hand between holes #11 and #12, I say, "Thank you for getting me out of the house tonight. I needed this more than you even know."

"You're welcome, Ryan," she smiles at me, her beautiful teeth glinting in the setting sun. "I enjoy spending time with you. Especially when I'm destroying you in mini-putt."

I move quickly and catch her off-guard, wrapping my arms around her waist, lifting her off the ground and carrying her over my shoulder toward the pond in the middle of the course. The water is green and full of dirt, scraps of paper and cigarette butts. She squeals, semi-fighting to escape my grasp.

"Ryan! No, Ryan! Please don't do it!" she shrieks, tugging at my arms and laughing so hard that she can barely breathe. I'm laughing too, knowing full well I'd never do it but enjoying torturing her.

I stand near the edge of the water, holding her while she squirms and squeals and laughs. "I won't do it if you'll say yes to my next question."

"Okay, okay, anything!"

"Will you come to my first pre-season game on Tuesday?"

Brenna stops squirming and looks at me. "You could have asked me anything and *that's* what you're asking?"

I jab my thumb into her ribs, tickling her. "You didn't say yes."

"Ryan! Yes, yes! I'll go!" I set her down and she smacks my arm lightly. "I would have said yes without you torturing me. Although I don't know jack shit about hockey, so..."

"So this weekend I'll teach you everything you need to know, and on Tuesday, I'll have a ticket waiting for you at Will Call."

Her smile is a mile wide and of course, that makes me smile, too. "Thank you. I am really excited for my first hockey game!"

"I'm excited to have you there, cheering me on." I need her there, more than she knows, and I'm thrilled that she's agreed to go.

It's amazing how just a few short hours ago, I was in such a dark place, and when I'm around Brenna... everything is light and full of hope. I've almost forgotten about the horrible things my dad said to me.

Almost.

14. BRENNA

Ryan has practice the next morning at 6am, so I stay in his bed for a little while after he leaves, soaking it all in. The sun's rays lazily cross the wall as the morning dawns. Birds chirp happily somewhere in the distance. The low hum of moving traffic is nearly absent out here in the suburbs and I realize I had all-but forgotten what the peace and quiet are actually like since I moved into the city. My entire body is sore from the marathon sex we had after we got home from mini-putt, but it's that wonderfully pleasant kind of sore from feeling so good for so long.

I've known Ryan for exactly one week and yet it feels like years. No one has made me laugh as hard as he has in far too long. I mean, Carly comes close, but she's my best friend, and as much as I love her, neither of us swing that way.

He makes me feel happy and safe. Even yesterday afternoon when he was a completely different man than the one I had seen before then, I was never afraid. I was anxious and confused, yes, but not afraid. Probably because he was behaving the exact same way I would if I had to spend three days with my family.

I eventually crawl out of Ryan's giant, plush bed, pull on my sleep tank and pajama shorts, and decide to explore the house a little. Most of Ryan's belongings are still in boxes, but I've noticed more items appearing here and there each time I'm at his house.

Ryan has a luxurious master bathroom off the bedroom, done in a beautiful light gray tile, complete with a giant whirlpool tub and waterfall shower. Two huge frosted glass window panes allow for plenty of natural light. There are more cabinets in this bathroom than in my entire kitchen.

I wander into the hallway and crack open the door to one of the other bedrooms. It is filled with cardboard boxes with various labels, but sitting in the middle is a single cardboard box, the flaps wide open. Slowly I walk inside and kneel in front of the box, curiosity getting the best of me.

On top of the pile is a stack of 4"x6" photographs. The first one is of Ryan and two guys from his team back in Philly in their jerseys, standing on the ice, grinning from ear to ear with their arms over each other's shoulders. Ryan looks incredibly young, so it must have been taken early in his career.

The next photo looks to have been taken around the same time, and features a fresh-faced Ryan, sitting at a large wooden desk in a fancy office, shaking hands with a very important looking guy in a suit and tie.

I continue flipping through the photos, many of them of Ryan on the ice at various games, some from press conferences and charity events, and others of him and teammates just hanging out.

At the bottom of the stack is a photo much older than the others. The edges of it are worn and frayed. In this photo, Ryan only looks to be about ten or eleven, and he's standing with a hockey stick in hand and a massive grin on his face next to a boy who looks like he's about fourteen years old. This other boy is an entire head taller than Ryan, and his hair is lighter in color and longer than Ryan's.

But his face looks almost exactly like Ryan's.

I flip the photo over and written on the back is:
Ryan and Sam Flynn, 2001.

Ryan has a brother? Why hasn't he mentioned him at all?

My cell phone starts ringing from the other room at that moment and I recognize the ringtone as Carly, so I quickly put the photos back in the box and run into the master bedroom. I can't even say hello before Carly starts screaming.

"Have you been online today!?"

"Carly? Uh, no? It's like 7:30 in the morning."

"Bren. There are photos of you and Ryan *everywhere* online."

My heart stops. I'm pretty sure I didn't hear her correctly. "What?"

"Yes! Apparently you guys went mini-putting last night?"

I pace across the room. "Yeah, we did." My hands are starting to shake.

"Well, now you're the hot gossip of the hockey world. Everyone is speculating online over who Ryan Flynn's first Chicago puck bunny is."

Instantly, my pulse skyrockets and my cheeks flush. "That's what they're saying? Are you fucking kidding me?"

"Don't go online, Bren. It's kind of a shitshow right now, but it'll be okay. It'll all blow over in a couple days and no one will even remember or care."

"Do any of the articles or whatever know who I actually am?"

"No, not yet." Somehow that makes me feel a little bit better. "Seriously Bren, it's no big deal." I know she's trying to minimize the situation, but it isn't working. "I at least wanted to make sure you knew."

"Thanks for letting me know, Carls." I stop pacing and stare out one of Ryan's bedroom windows. His backyard is bare minus a couple small trees in one corner of the lot. "You're right, it isn't a big deal. It'll die down soon. I should probably text Ryan and let him know, though."

"Sure thing," Carly replies. "I'll keep posting nasty comments on these gossip sites in the meantime."

"Carly," I say sternly.

"I'm only sort-of kidding, Bren. Anyway, let me know if you need anything. You know, ice cream, shotgun, whatever. I'm your girl."

I roll my eyes. "Thanks. Talk to you later." I hang up and, flopping back down on his bed, immediately type out a text to Ryan, *Call me as soon as you're done at practice. It's urgent.*

I read over it and realize that, maybe to him, this won't be a big deal. After all, he's been photographed with loads of puck bunnies in the past. I don't want to make a mountain out of a molehill, so I retype my message to *Hey, FYI – Someone took photos of us last night at mini-putt and put them online. Just thought you should know.* It sounds a lot more calm than I'm feeling so I roll with it and hit send.

With a sigh, I try to put my phone down and forget about it – but I can't. I need to see the photos for myself. Of course, they aren't difficult to find. "Who is Ryan Flynn's Chicago Mystery Woman?" and "Flynn on the Prowl in New City Weeks After Trade" are only a couple of the headlines I see. Some of the sites speculate that I'm a puck bunny from Wisconsin, upgrading from the minors to the major league. A couple bloggers are convinced that I'm a well-known bunny named Liz from Arizona going incognito in Chicago.

As mortifying, degrading and frustrating as the situation is, I can't help but notice how absolutely adorable Ryan and I look in the photos. In one shot, I'm bent over, about to putt, and he's standing behind me, his muscled, tattooed arms crossed over his chest, wearing a smirk. In another, he's holding me over the edge of the water and we're both laughing. In one more, we're kissing passionately at Hole #18 after I beat him by almost 20 strokes. His hands are on my lower back, pulling me in close to him, and my arms are wrapped around his neck. We look carefree and happy; such a stark contrast to only a few hours before the photos were taken.

I think back to the Ryan that opened the door yesterday afternoon. What did his father do to him to have caused such a drastic change in his entire personality? I get weird when I'm forced to spend time with my family, but nowhere near the level Ryan reached.

Who is this fascinating, mysterious, sexy guy, and what are the secrets that he's hiding?

15. RYAN

"Mother fucker," I grumble as I scroll through one of the gossip sites that is, unfortunately, posting photos and speculations of me and my "mystery woman." I saw Brenna's text as soon as I got out of the shower in the locker room after a particularly tough practice. I turn to Nils, who is occupying the locker next to me, and show him the headline. "Who comes up with this shit anyway?"

"Jealous people?" he says in his thick Swedish accent with a shrug as he towels off from his shower. He and I have been getting paired up in practices lately, and we click pretty well. He's shorter than I am, but he's one of the fastest guys in the entire league right now, and I don't stand a chance of keeping up with his speed. Luckily, my puck handling skills are better than his, so we complement each other well on the ice. "You've been in the

96

league longer than I have. Shouldn't you be used to the gossip by now?"

"But Brenna isn't a puck bunny," I grit out. I toss my phone up on the ledge in my locker. "She's cool, man. She's not like those thirsty bitches. She's real."

Nils throws his towel in his gym bag and pulls on a pair of boxers. "If you can't handle the media then it won't work out anyway, no?"

I pause partway through pulling on my shorts and stare at Nils. "I never said I can't handle it."

"I believe you," he says, not looking in my direction. He adjusts the waistband of his athletic shorts. "But can *she* handle it?"

I stare at the pale green carpet under my feet. "I don't know. It's too soon to tell for sure, I guess." Damn him. He might be five years younger than me, but he's a smart dude. "I hope she can handle it. I really like this girl, Nils."

"You've got it bad," he smirks at me. I can only smile in return. Of course, as Nils leaves the locker room and I turn my attention back to my phone, the smile slips away. She sounds calm in her message, but what if she's freaking out? What if she isn't at the house when I go back there?

I don't think I've ever gotten dressed so fast.

"Brenna?" I call into the house as I step into the foyer. "Brenna, are you here?"

"In the kitchen," she calls back. I breathe a sigh of relief as I toss my bag down and walk toward the sound of her voice.

She's at the island, spreading mayonnaise on a piece of bread. "Hi, Ryan," she says softly, hesitant. She sets down the knife and turns to face me, wringing her hands. She looks so beautiful and natural standing in my kitchen, but everything feels... awkward?

My mind is freaking out. "Hey Brenna," I try to say as evenly as possible. "Ah- are you okay?"

"Yeah, I'm okay," she says with a smile that doesn't quite reach her eyes.

"Hey, it's okay," I tell her, crossing the kitchen and taking her into my arms. She softens under my embrace. "It's no big deal."

"It feels like a big deal," she sighs against my chest. Then she looks up at me with those chocolate brown eyes and something moves inside me. "I know you're famous and all, but I guess I didn't realize that meant if we went out in public, we'd end up being the hot gossip of the entire league."

I squeeze her gently and Brenna buries her face into my shirt. "I'm sorry I didn't warn you. I didn't think about it, to be honest. It's been a long time since I've taken a girl out in public like that before."

"Really?" She looks up at me again, curious.

"Yeah. The last time I had a steady girlfriend was my second year in the league." Michelle was nice enough, but she

98

couldn't handle the grueling travel schedule of the NHL. We only dated for half the season before she called it quits. I had really liked her. After she bailed, I went a little crazy and went on a bit of a bunny-fucking spree. I'm pretty sure I boned anything with tits that breathed for a while there. Not my proudest moment, that's for sure.

Brenna shifts her weight from one foot to the other, her body still pressed against mine. "The last thing I wanted to do is be a distraction to you or bring stress into your life..."

"You're not, though," I say, squeezing her again. "I can handle this. But I need to make sure *you* are okay."

She's quiet for a moment, then says "What are we, exactly?"

"You mean our relationship?"

"Yeah."

I release her and scratch my head. "I mean, I really like you, Brenna. I don't know if I've made that obvious or not, but I think you're really cool."

"I think you're cool too," she says. "And I really like you as well. But I guess... I guess I need some clarity. I need this – whatever we have – to be defined." She shifts, visibly uncomfortable as she searches for the right words. "I don't know if I can do... casual."

She looks so small and meek. And adorable. "I'd like to continue to see you." I run a hand across her cheek. She leans into the touch. "But this will be hard, Brenna. My schedule is...

intense, to say the least. I'll be gone a LOT and for long stretches of time through the season. And the articles today? There will be more of them. A lot of them will say that I'm cheating on you when I'm not. That's how life in the league is. If we're going to keep seeing each other, I need to know that you're in this for the long haul."

She closes her eyes, my hand cupping her face, and lets out a soft breath. Then her eyes open and they're sparkling. "Okay. I'm in." She smiles, and my arms go around her as I kiss her. I rest my forehead against hers so we're nose-to-nose. "Thank you."

"For what?" I ask her.

"For giving me everything I need. And not freaking out because I needed to know that we're on the same page."

I pull back so I can better stare into her eyes. She tilts her head inquisitively. "You thought I would freak out because you wanted to know if we were going to exclusively date each other?"

Brenna's eyes avert mine, her gaze tracing the tile on the floor. She chews on her lip. "Well... yeah."

I take her face in both my hands and gently lift her chin towards me until her eyes meet mine. "Why?"

She sighs. "My ex kind of fucked with my head." She pulls away from me, picking up the lid to the mayonnaise jar and screwing it on. She moves to the fridge to put it away.

"He must have really fucked with you, if you honestly thought I'd be upset."

Brenna straightens and shuts the refrigerator door, shaved ham in hand. "Well, Ashton wouldn't commit to me. He strung me along for the better part of eight years so, yeah, I'd say he fucked me up pretty good."

My jaw drops. "Eight years?"

"Give or take." She puts the ham on top of several slices of bread. "We dated on and off through college and a bit afterwards, but he always kept me at arms length. I was in love with him, but... he just saw me as a piece of ass and someone to manipulate. I haven't seen him in over a year – not since I found out he has a fiancée."

"Wow," I say. A lot of things are suddenly starting to make sense. "No wonder you've been so guarded and unsure of me."

She hands me a plate with two sandwiches on it. "Yeah," she says softly. "It's hard to trust again after going through all the shit Ashton put me through. But I think I'm ready to try, if you're still willing to give me a chance."

"Give you a chance? Brenna, you aren't damaged goods, if that's what you're thinking." Her face confirms that I'm right on target. I set my plate down on the island and, taking her by surprise, kiss her passionately. I pour every ounce of feeling I have for this girl into my lips and tongue, and I feel her melt in my hands.

Whatever this Ashton fucker did to her – I want to fix it. She deserves the world, and I'm going to give it to her.

16. BRENNA

Tuesday's preseason game starts at 7pm. I know if I try to go home to the north end of the city before going to the game, I'll have a heck of a time getting back across Chicago to the arena on the south side by the time the game starts. I don't want to miss a minute of the action, even if I don't fully understand what is happening.

Ryan spent the weekend trying to teach me what icing and offsides are using youtube videos for reference. It helped, but I don't think I'll fully understand a lot of the rules of the game until I get a few of them under my belt.

I show up to work on Tuesday morning in my typical blouse and dress slacks, but I brought a bag with a more casual outfit for the game. Of course, with this being my first hockey game ever, I didn't own anything of the Velocity, but thankfully

Carly let me borrow one of her t-shirts with the team logo on the front. I paired it with dark skinny jeans and grey ankle boots.

However, when I get into my office, a small package wrapped in white paper with a red bow on top is sitting on my desk. Natalie follows me into my office, obviously having spotted the unexpected delivery. I drop my purse and bag of clothes in my desk drawer and settle into my chair, eyeing the package. Natalie perches herself on the edge of my desk, looking giddy.

The gift tag attached to the present merely reads *Can't wait to see you in this tonight.*

"It's gotta be lingerie from your mystery guy!" Natalie squawks. "And you told me it wasn't serious! Is he into red? I bet that explains the bow!"

I unwrap the paper and toss it into the trash. When I pull back the cardboard flaps and peek inside, I'm shocked to find a red Velocity jersey inside. On the back is FLYNN and his number, 25.

Natalie is confused. "Does your mystery guy have a hockey fetish?"

"He *is* a hockey player," I say with a soft smile. I haven't taken my eyes off the jersey. I'm sure it was no big deal for Ryan to get a jersey with his name and number on it for me, but to me, it's a big deal. First of all, I don't have enough money to buy a Velocity t-shirt, let alone a jersey, because after looking online I discovered how shockingly expensive they are. But in addition to that, he wants me to wear something of his, possibly even to be identified *as* his.

It's simultaneously amazing and terrifying.

Natalie is chattering away in my ear but I'm not listening to a word she's saying. My mind has drifted to tonight and the fact that I'll be watching my boyfriend do what he does best while wearing I'm his jersey.

Ryan had already told me I wouldn't hear from him at all until after the game because of morning practice, a game-day nap, and then his warm up and prep routine prior to puck drop. Today, the work day just can't go fast enough for me.

The concourse is buzzing with energy and excitement as I pick up my ticket at the will call window at the arena. It's a little overwhelming and I'm not sure where to go. I decide to hit one of the food vendors first, grabbing a hot dog and a beer. They're overpriced, but I didn't have time to grab anything else on the way from work, so it will have to do. I stroll past the team store, where fans are browsing a selection of anything and everything Velocity branded, before going to find my seat.

When I emerge from the hallway into the arena between the upper and lower sections, I'm stunned by the size of this place. Tens of thousands of seats line the bowl-shaped arena. Several flags hang from the rafters, honoring famous players and denoting the four times the Chicago Velocity have won the coveted Stanley Cup Championship.

One of the ushers, clad in a black suit with a Velocity lapel pin, notices my expression and comes over to help me find my seat. "You've got a great seat," he says as he glances at my ticket. "Follow me, miss," He leads me down the stairs into the lower section of the arena and into a seat in the middle of a row, about 10 rows back from the ice, with a direct view across the rink to the Velocity bench.

I settle in and eat my hot dog, absorbing the scene around me. Fans file into the arena, and a lot of scantily-clad women gather near the glass at the edge of the ice, anxious to see the players coming out to warm up.

I feel my phone vibrate in my pocket. Confused, I pull it out and see that I have five unread messages from Ashton.

B, I miss you.

Who are you with right now? Why don't you ever text me back?

You have no right to still be mad at me, B.

After all of your shit I dealt with, we are even now.

You know you're still in love with me.

I stare at my phone, unsure of what to think. I finally type back *Why do you keep messaging me? You're with Jenny now.*

He immediately replies. *You and I both know that we are not done. I'm willing to give you another chance even though you don't deserve it.*

My heart jumps into my throat when I spot Ryan coming onto the ice over the top of my phone screen. He moves gracefully in a circle around one side of the rink with the rest of his team. His helmet is off, the longer top part of his hair blowing behind him as he moves. The way he skates across the ice looks effortless and natural and I've never been so in awe of someone's grace before. My phone and Ashton are forgotten about, for now.

The goalie breaks off out of the circle and heads to the front of the net while the rest of the team splits off into two groups near the "blue line" (which, much to my surprise, is literally a blue line cutting across the ice) and they begin handling pucks. I watch a couple of the guys showing off, flipping pucks up into the air and catching them on the ends of their sticks.

"Hey, where did you manage to get a Flynn jersey already?" says a voice from next to me. I glance over and standing at the end of my row are two busty blondes. One is wearing thigh-high black leather boots and tiny denim shorts, and the one who is talking to me has a plunging red minidress that barely covers her ass.

"Oh, um, it was given to me as a gift," I say, wringing my hands nervously.

"Lucky," says the girl with the boots. "Ryan Flynn is my favorite player. I moved here from Philly so I could follow him." The way she enunciates the word *favorite* rubs me the wrong way. These two must be puck bunnies.

"I would do anything to fuck Ryan Flynn," says the first girl. I have to restrain myself from rolling my eyes.

"Can you believe some chick was already seen with him?" Boots girl whines at me. "I mean, seriously? She wasn't even that pretty." She flips her bleached hair over her shoulder. I can only nod in agreement and pray that neither of them suddenly recognize me.

Thankfully, they squeal and teeter down the stairs to the edge of the glass as one of the guys from the team stops and waves to fans. I'm pretty sure minidress girl shoves her cleavage up against the glass as the player skates by.

Ryan eventually sits near the center of the rink and starts to stretch. I watch his eyes flick up to me, a smile lining his face as his gaze meets mine. My heart beats thunderously in my chest and I grin at him, pointing to my jersey. He nods his head in acknowledgment and I can't see or hear anything around me but him. This moment – and the connection we share – is indescribable.

The seats around me begin to fill up as warm-up winds down and the teams head back into their respective locker rooms. Two women, a mother and her twenty-something daughter, sit on one side of me, but the seat on the opposite side of me remains empty. There are many empty seats throughout the arena but Ryan told me that is normal for pre-season games.

After player introductions, the national anthem, and the puck is dropped, the game begins with the Velocity facing off against the Dallas Spurs. The ladies next to me, whose names are Theresa and Morgan, help explain to me what is happening throughout the game.

At the end of the first period, the score is tied 0-0. Ryan played a few good shifts but the defense of the Spurs was too strong to get through.

Theresa turns to me as many of the spectators leave their seats for potty breaks and refills. "So this is your first hockey game, you said?"

"Yep, sure is."

"This section is mainly season ticket holders or families of the team." She says, smiling at me. "Which are you?"

"Uh, well, my boyfriend is on the team," I say quietly, not wanting to be overheard. I'd rather not be identified by anyone.

"Ahh," Theresa's eyes sparkle. "I'm guessing by your jersey that Flynn is the lucky guy?" I nod, trying to hold my smile back from becoming a full-on grin. I've only just met Theresa and Morgan, but they both seem so nice.

"Are you season ticket holders?" I ask them. They both shake their heads and Morgan speaks up.

"Patrick Huff – the Captain – is my older brother."

"Wow!" I exclaim. "That's really cool! Do you come to every game?"

"I come to most of them," Morgan says. Her short black hair is cut into a stylish bob. "My mom here comes to a few a year since she lives up in Minnesota. But Patrick has these two seats reserved for every game, so if my Mom can't come then I'll usually bring a friend."

"That's really cool." The teams come racing back onto the ice, and fans start to settle back into their seats for the second period of the game.

Halfway through the second period, Ryan is on the ice. He is charging toward the Spurs' goalie, guiding the puck with precision. While looking directly at the goalie, he winds up and slaps it to his left where another Chicago player, Nils Larsson, is waiting. Nils' shot rockets past the goalie and straight into the net.

Theresa and Morgan immediately jump to their feet and cheer along with the rest of the fans in our section. I take the cue and stand up too, clapping and yelling along with them as the entire arena is filled with cheering, music, and the blasting of what sounds like a cruise ship horn, which apparently happens after every goal scored by the home team in their arena.

Nils and Ryan skate to each other and are crushed into a group hug by the other Velocity players on the ice in celebration. Once they break apart, Ryan's eyes find mine and his grin is a mile wide. I bounce happily on the balls of my feet, swept up in the cheering of the crowd.

Eventually, the celebration dies down and the players prepare for the next drop of the puck, so we return to our seats. I notice Theresa grinning at me.

"Your boy got an assist!" she says to me.

"I don't really know what that means, but I'm going to assume it's a good thing."

She laughs and slaps me on the shoulder. "You'll get the hang of this soon enough, kiddo."

Before I know it, the game is over and the Velocity have won, 2-1. Fans high-five each other on the way out of the arena, talking about how great the team is going to be this season. Even the fans of the Spurs seem somewhat happy despite losing. Hockey is kind of a weird sport, I've decided.

I start to leave, bidding goodbye to Theresa and Morgan, but Morgan grabs my hand. "Aren't you going to go say hello to your man?"

"Uhh, I figured I just meet him at home when he's done?" I say, feeling dumb. Ryan didn't tell me what to do or where to go after the game was over.

"Come on, follow me," she says. They lead me up the stairs to the main concourse, and then through a set of doors to one side leading to another set of stairs, this time going down. At the bottom of those stairs are two of the suit-clad guys, each holding a clipboard.

Morgan and Theresa pull out their IDs, and I follow suit, handing it to one of the men. He looks me over and scans my ID, then glances over the page on his clipboard. "Welcome, Miss Wilson." He hands my ID back to me and I quickly tuck it back into my wallet before following Morgan and Theresa through a doorway.

Inside the door is a large room filled with many couches and various chairs and coffee tables. There are quite a few people already in the room, a lot of them around my age or younger, some with a small child or two in tow.

"This is the family waiting area," Morgan tells me. The three of us take a seat on one of the couches. "We get to chill in here, away from the crowds, until the guys are done being interviewed and showering and stuff."

"Good thing Ryan had your name on the list," Theresa giggles. "Although I suppose we could have always said you were with us. The security guys here all know us pretty well."

A few of the other hockey moms come over and chat with Theresa. Morgan scrolls through her phone, looking bored. I suppose after growing up in this world, it would be just another day in the family waiting area, but I'm completely out of my element, so I look around, scoping out the place and also people-watching.

A lot of the hockey WAGs – which I learned through one of the gossip sites means Wives and Girlfriends - look like fucking supermodels. One of them struts by in four-inch heels and I swear I've seen her on the cover of a magazine or something.

"So I actually met Ryan the other day," Morgan tells me out of nowhere. I turn my attention to her. "Pat brought him in to the bar I work at last week. Nice guy. How did you meet each other?"

"Uhh, well..." I drop my voice, looking toward to Theresa to make sure she isn't listening. Thankfully, she's absorbed in conversation with a couple of the other moms. "It's kind of embarrassing. Promise you won't tell anyone?"

"Pinky-swear," she says with a wink. We lock pinkies and both giggle.

"Okay, well, I was out for my best friend's engagement party, and feeling a little down because all of our friends are engaged or married now except me, so when this guy started hitting on me at the bar... well..."

"Shut up," Morgan says, her eyes wide. "You probably didn't even know who he was, did you?"

"I didn't have a clue," I admit, wringing my hands. "So this is a whole new world for me. I had never even seen hockey on tv until this past weekend."

Morgan sits back into the couch. "That's crazy, and pretty cool. I mean, what are the chances of finding your possible future spouse at a bar?"

"I wouldn't go *that* far yet," I say. I would never admit to her that the word spouse sent a chill down my spine.

"Regardless," she says with a wave of her hand. "It gives me hope that I'll meet someone someday."

"Aw, you will," I touch her shoulder softly.

"Yeah, well, if my super overprotective brother would lay off, that would probably help." She rolls her eyes. "At least he

113

cares about me, I guess, but I wish he'd show it in a different way."

A bunch of the players finally emerge from the doorway at the end of the room, freshly showered and dressed in their suits and ties, Ryan included. I stand up as he comes over to me, a huge smile on both of our faces.

I'm not sure what he's going to do when he reaches me, but I'm pleasantly surprised when he wraps his arms around me and lifts me to his level before sealing his mouth over mine. I wrap my arms around his neck, sinking into the kiss but still aware that we're surrounded by his new teammates and their families. Thankfully he's aware too and we break apart, smiling.

"Lets get out of here," he growls into my ear. Instantly, my skin is covered in goosebumps and I feel the heat of need between my legs. This man's voice does wonders to me.

I say goodbye to Morgan and Theresa, and Ryan nearly drags me to the exit doors without any hesitation.

.

17. RYAN

I had a great first game with my new team. I'm still learning my new teammates skills, strengths, and quirks, but Coach has had me on a line with Nils all week, and that guy and I connect really well. I'm stoked that I got an assist on a great feed to him tonight. He's so fast, and combined with my puck-handling skills, I think we can make a good pair for the Velocity going forward.

Yeah, I didn't get a ton of ice time tonight, but I also didn't expect to. At least I made the most of what I did get.

Take that, Ryan-from-last-season. I'm a new man on a new team now. Maybe a fresh start is just what I needed.

Seeing Brenna in the stands, cheering me on, wearing the jersey I got for her, was so indescribable in the best way. I get to see her be beautiful and smart and sexy all the time, especially when she talks about her job, but this was the first time she got to see me do what I do best.

I won't ever get to have the opportunity to see my brother or mom in the stands. My dad hasn't come to a game since before Sam died. So at this point, I just appreciate my fans, and live vicariously through my teammates who don't have fucked up pasts like I do.

But I swear to god, I played even better just by knowing that Brenna was there at the game. It was hard not to just stare at her in the stands, or revel in her looking around the arena in awe and wonderment. Her innocence, naivete, and sheer interest in what I do is addicting. Sharing this part of myself with someone I care about... there's nothing like it. I find myself wanting her to be at every game I play.

"Take off your pants, but leave the jersey on," I command her after we get back to my house, my voice huskier than normal. I toss my suit jacket onto the back of the couch in the living room. "I'll meet you in the bedroom." I kiss the tip of her nose, and, as she turns to head to the bedroom, I swat her ass. She gasps and sticks her tongue out at me as she rounds the corner.

I head into the kitchen and grab a sports drink out of the fridge. I'm going to need the extra electrolytes tonight. I down half of it while leaning against the island, taking a moment to relax. Except for my cock, that is, which is already straining against the zipper of my suit pants.

Something about this girl fires me up like no other.

I unbutton my suit pants and hastily pull them off, tossing them onto the countertop, followed by my socks. I loosened my tie in the car, so I easily undo it, pull it from my collar and throw it on top of the pants. The buttons on my shirt are next to be undone, and it, as well as the white t-shirt underneath, top off the pile.

Clad in nothing but my black boxer-briefs, I walk into the bedroom, and am greeted with the wonderful sight of Brenna wearing only the jersey, just like I requested of her. It barely skims the tops of her thighs, hardly covering her ass at all. Her smooth legs are a mile long coming out from under the red material.

She walks over to me, slowly, seductively. It's a side of Brenna I haven't seen before, but I'm loving it. Once she's standing in front of me, her smoldering eyes lock with mine, and she slowly sinks before me to her knees.

The little bit of blood that was still in my head rushes to my dick at breakneck speed. I had a different plan for this evening's activities, but instead her sudden confidence and power have me instantly filled with the overwhelming need for her lips to be on my cock.

Her hands glide up the backs of my legs, squeezing my ass before moving upward and gripping the waistband of my boxer-briefs. She begins to remove them, tantalizing in the way she glides the fabric over my stiff cock and down my thighs. Her nails lightly scratch my skin as they go, rocketing shudders of desire through me.

As she wraps a hand around the shaft of my dick, I moan her name.

When she takes the head of it into her wet mouth, I almost lose it right then and there.

I need to get it together. I'm not fifteen and getting a blowy for the first damn time.

She flicks her tongue over the sensitive head, tracing the grooves and edges. One hand cups my balls, and she rolls them around in her palm, her other hand gripping the side of my thigh, nails digging in.

Slowly, she takes more of me into her mouth, teasing me as I watch myself glide in and out from between her luscious lips. I ball my left hand into a fist and bring it to my mouth, biting down on my fingers to keep from careening over the edge too soon.

She starts to hum while she licks and sucks, shooting electric waves of pleasure to every extremity on me. Still biting my left hand, I grab the back of her head with my right, fisting her hair as my hips and her mouth move in rhythm.
Brenna looks up at me, with heavy-lidded, chocolate eyes, her mouth stretched over my throbbing cock, her long, blonde hair flowing over her shoulders, and the thought crosses my mind for the first time:

I could fall in love with this woman.

I let go, and the orgasm takes me. I'm soaring through the sky on fiery wings of pleasure as I empty myself inside her mouth. This is without a doubt one of the best orgasms I've ever had. Brenna holds on through the whole thing, draining every last pulse from me before rocking back on her heels and swallowing with a small shudder.

"Oh man, you didn't have to do that," I tell her, running a hand through my hair.

She smiles at me. "I wanted to. It's really not that bad. Any girl that says it is, is lying to you."

Groaning, I lean down and kiss her roughly. "You're the coolest girl ever, you know that?" Her grin is contagious. I offer her my hand and pull her to her feet and into my arms. I'm sweaty as fuck, but she doesn't seem to care.

"Congratulations on your first game as part of the Chicago Velocity," she says, pulling the jersey over her head. Suddenly, I'm finding myself ready for round two.

18. BRENNA

Carly had been dropping hints for days, but she eventually starts begging me to let her meet Ryan after his game on Tuesday.

Come on Bren! Bring him to the house for dinner with me and John! I promise I'll behave :)

Ryan snatches my phone out of my hand and reads the message before I can grab it back.

"Carly promises she'll behave, eh?" he says, his Canadian accent sneaking out along with a smirk. "You aren't ashamed to bring me around your friends, are you?"

"More like I'm afraid to bring my friends around you," I quip, making another attempt to grab my phone back from him. Of course, he easily dodges. I sigh at him. "Do you want to have dinner with Carly and John?"

Ryan kisses the tip of my nose and hands my phone back to me. "Only if you want to."

I stare at the screen, contemplating for a moment and planning around Ryan's preseason schedule. He has his first away game on Friday night, and a home game on Monday. I type back *Okay, you win. We will see you Sunday at 6. No funny business!*

Ryan pulls up in front of the house at 6pm sharp and puts the car in park. He hurries around the car, shutting the door of his Audi behind me. I still can't get over all the tiny gestures he does for me. Either he's well-versed in wooing women, or he is genuinely a nice guy. I'm finding myself really hoping it's the latter of the two that is true.

Carly opens the door before we even reach the steps, wearing a giant smile and her bright pink apron. "You must be Ryan!" she squeals, reaching out to Ryan and pulling him into a hug.

"And you must be Carly," he laughs somewhat uncomfortably, lightly patting her shoulders in the saddest excuse for hugging her back. He shoots me a questioning smile.

"Sorry, I should have warned you," I say quickly. "Carly is a hugger."

Carly finally releases Ryan and motions us inside. "Come in, come in. John is pulling the lasagna out of the oven."

I follow Carly and Ryan in through the front door and the wonderful aroma of pasta and garlic bread teases my nose. John comes out of our tiny kitchen, pulling off an oven mitt to shake Ryan's hand.

John is tall and lean, and handsome in his own right, but he looks boyish next to Ryan's broad shoulders and rugged features. I take a moment, standing back and admiring Ryan as he talks with John. He looks absolutely stunning in a black button-up shirt with the sleeves rolled up, showing off a portion of the tattoos that wrap around his arms all the way from the top of his shoulders to the backs of his hands. His dark jeans fit him perfectly, highlighting his wonderfully sculpted ass. Ryan's hair is styled in his trademark mess; his beard expertly tamed in contrast. His smile is the best part of all, though: It makes our tiny, dingy home feel bright and airy.

I can't believe I get to call this man my boyfriend.

"Holy. Shit," Carly whispers next to me. "He's even more gorgeous in person."

"I know," I say softly. "I'm still in shock."

Carly wraps her arms around me and says, almost so quietly that I almost miss it, "I can't wait to hear all about the crazy hot sex you've been having with him."

"What are you two whispering about?" John calls over to us. My cheeks are burning and Carly just laughs.

"Come on, let's get you a drink," Carly says, linking her arm through mine and pulling me around the guys and into the kitchen. She reaches into the back cabinet and pulls out the bottle of expensive sparkling wine we went halfsies on and have been saving for two years for 'a special occasion'. When I start to protest, she cuts me off with, "We're celebrating, Bren. I can't think of a better occasion than this."

"We didn't even crack it open when you got engaged!" I balk.

Carly ignores me and pops the cork over the sink, some of the foam spilling over the lip of the bottle. She smiles at me. "No, we didn't. So let's celebrate both occasions together! My engagement, and your new relationship."

I reach into the cabinet for four glasses. Our glassware, like nearly everything else in the entire house, is mismatched and came from a secondhand store. I feel my hands shaking slightly as I set the glasses on the Formica countertop.

John slides in next to her in the cramped kitchen to grab a spatula for the lasagna, which means I have to slide out of the kitchen so he can get in there. I walk around the tiny table we have set up dividing the kitchen from the living room and find Ryan staring at the photos we have hung on the walls.

Most of the photos around the house are Carly's. She has a huge collage frame up with probably close to 30 different photos in it of all kinds of important events in her life - there's ones of her as a kid with her two brothers and one sister, ones of her playing softball in middle and high school, receiving awards in high school, graduating college, and photos of her hanging out with tons of friends, some of whom I know and some I don't. Then she has another collage frame filled with photos of just her and John which is nauseatingly cute and such a Carly thing to have.

Then there's my photos. I have two frames. One is a photo of Carly and I on campus shortly after we met. We're both sitting on a bench and laughing at something Carly had said. The other frame holds a photo of me and my Dad, from when I was only 6 or 7 years old. It's from before everything got all fucked up, which is the only reason I keep it on display.

Ryan admires our decor, and I fidget, anxious over what he is thinking. Is he surprised at how tiny and run-down our house is? Are he and John hitting it off? Is Carly going to be too much for him to handle?

"Not very many photos of you up here," he murmurs, quiet enough that Carly and John won't hear.

"No need," I sigh. "No friends and no family, so nothing to hang up."

He pulls his phone out of his back pocket and slides over to me, putting an arm around my shoulder. "You have me," Ryan says with a smile. "We will just have to take some photos for you to hang up." He holds his phone away from us and snaps a photo. He's smiling at the camera, eyes bright and 1000 watt smile at full strength. I look disheveled and plain next to him, but he seems to think that the photo looks good because he immediately texts it to me.

"Time for a toast!" Carly yells, thrusting one of the glasses of sparkling wine into my hand. John calmly hands one to Ryan.

"What are we toasting to?" Ryan asks Carly, his eyes sparkling with amusement.

"To Bren finally getting a boyfriend and getting out of the house for a change!" she shouts. I groan audibly, my discomfort at this whole situation evolving to irritation. "And to John and I getting engaged."

"Cheers!" We all tink our glasses together in the middle of the living room. As Ryan tips his glass back, his eyes are locked on me.

19. RYAN

John's lasagna is incredible. I know I'm going to regret it tomorrow, but it's still preseason. Fuck my diet for one night.

"This is fantastic, John," I gush over my third piece.

"Thanks, man," John says and takes a drink from his glass. "I think I may have missed my calling in the culinary field."

Carly places her hand on John's and runs her thumb over his. "That's okay, baby. I get your cooking all to myself." Carly grins. "Well, okay, I guess I'm forced to share your cooking with Bren for a little while longer."

The room is uncomfortably quiet until Brenna clears her throat. She's focused straight down at her plate, lips pursed and flush creeping into her cheeks. Carly is oblivious to this fact. Sensing the awkwardness, John stands to clear away plates, making as much noise as possible.

I place my hand on Brenna's shoulder. "Are you ready to leave soon?" I ask her gently. She nods, avoiding my eyes. I know I need to expedite our exit because she's upset. She's been on edge all night anyway, probably just from being nervous about letting me into her home and her life, but now she's visibly upset. I help John clear the table while Carly flits around the kitchen, packing up leftovers and humming a pop tune.

With a firm handshake, I thank John for the excellent meal and bid him farewell. Brenna waves goodbye to her friends from the doorway and rushes out into the evening. I quickly follow after her.

She's waiting by the car, squinting against the sun hanging low in the sky. It reflects off the metal and glass, amplified by each surface.

I'd like to think it's the sunlight causing tears to form in her eyes, but I read her too well. We're barely buckled into the car before I turn and say to her, "Talk to me, Brenna."

A tear trickles down her cheek. She sucks in a shaky breath. "Carly just has no clue sometimes."

I pull away from the curb and start toward home. "What do you mean?"

"She's 'forced' to share John's cooking with me?" Brenna says angrily, staring out the window. She scoffs. "What a rude thing to say about your best friend."

"Maybe she meant it as a joke?" I offer.

127

"Carly tries to 'joke' sometimes, but when she does, she's really saying exactly how she feels about something." Brenna is quiet for a moment as I pull onto the freeway. The tears have stopped. "She says it's fine that we live together and all that, but then she makes jabs that she and John have no privacy, and that she feels bad that she'll be getting married and moving out and I'll be all alone in a place we can hardly afford together, let alone by myself."

I'm quiet for a minute, processing what she's said. "I'm sure she has your best interests at heart, but it sounds like she's a little rough around the edges with showing that love and care to you."

"Maybe," Brenna says softly. "Or maybe we really are too different."

"What do you mean?"

"I mean that we are polar opposites. She's outgoing and beautiful and has a thousand friends and a super supportive family, and I am just me. No friends, zero family, broke as a joke, plain as hell, boring Brenna."

"You know that isn't true, Brenna." I look at her and smile quickly before focusing back on the road. "You're beautiful and spunky and you're MY friend. My more-than-friend. My girlfriend."

She glances at me, finally. "I don't understand what you see in me. Or what anyone sees in me."

I feel an ache in my chest. I wish so badly that I wasn't on the fucking Dan Ryan Expressway and could hold her in my arms right now. "Brenna. I promise I will show you everything I see in you. I'll help you to see it in yourself. I promise." I hold her slender hand in mine the rest of the way home.

I lay in bed later that night, my arm around Brenna who is asleep and curled into a ball next to me, and reflect on the evening.

When we arrived, I had immediately noticed how tiny the house was. It was one of those that is in a row of houses that look exactly like it and line both sides of the street for countless blocks. I know Carly and Brenna rent the place, and that it was ideal because of price and the proximity to the hospital Carly works at. Good thing it's only a rental though because the paint is chipping, the foundation is cracked, and parking in that part of the city is a living nightmare.

John and I talked for a bit when we arrived. I can tell he was in awe of being in the presence of an NHLer but was trying very hard to keep his cool. Carly, on the other hand, had no qualms about showing her excitement to be meeting me. As conceited as it sounds, you do get somewhat immune to the attention, to an extent. However, it is still flattering when someone says how big of a fan they are of yours.

Carly really upset Brenna tonight, but I think it was more that this was the straw that broke the camel's back instead of being the sole cause. I think Brenna was already stressing about me being in her house and meeting her friends, and I bet she and

Carly already had some kind of tension going on, and tonight it just all came to a head for her.

I want to prove to Brenna how amazing she truly is. I don't understand how she could think so minimally of herself. Every day I get closer with her. We haven't known each other for long but I already feel myself opening up to her, enjoying being with her and not being bored or annoyed with her presence.

But what has this girl been through to completely decimate her confidence?

She rustles next to me, groaning softly in her sleep as she shifts on the bed next to me. I rub my thumb over her bare shoulder and vow to myself that I will help Brenna to see herself exactly how I see her.

20. RYAN

"Hey Flynn!" Patrick calls at me from across the locker room. "My mom said you reserved the seats next to her and Morgan for the season, and last game she met your girl?"

I pull the boot of my skate over my foot. "Yeah man. Brenna said she had a great time with them at the last game, so I decided to make those my reserved seats for the year. Is that cool?"

"Of course," Patrick pulls his jersey over his head. "I'm glad for Morgs. She could really use a friend that's a girl around here." He glares around the locker room and I notice a couple of the guys duck their heads and avoid his gaze. "She's got enough MALES trying to be her friend," he says pointedly.

"It's good for Brenna too," I say. "She knew nothing about hockey until about 2 weeks ago, so getting her in with some of the Velocity women will be good." I tie the laces on my skate and stand up, making sure they're laced tight enough.

"You should tell your sister to not get too close with Flynn's girl. With his track record, this girl won't be around for long," a voice says from behind me. I turn around and it's coming from Corey Daniels, our backup goalie.

Corey Daniels used to be the Velocity's primary goalie until last season when Mitch Perry got called up from the minors because Corey was out with a groin injury and the Velocity's normal second goalie, Landon Jacobi, was out for hand surgery. Mitch had an amazing season and when Landon was healed up and back in, Coach kept playing Mitch instead of Corey.

"Shut the fuck up, Daniels," I mutter.

"What, Flynn, am I wrong?" He's taller than me by about four inches and easily has 30 pounds on me, but I could probably still take him down. Goalies have lightning quick reflexes but I'm pretty quick myself.

"Yeah, actually, you are," I am standing only a few inches from him now. "Brenna is different."

"So you're telling all of us that notorious hockey playboy Ryan Flynn is a one-woman kind of man now?" Corey spits on the floor. "Bullshit. You'll cheat on her before regular season even starts."

I feel my blood boiling and fight to hold back. I'm the newcomer on this team, fighting for my chance to stay in the NHL, and I need to not fuck it up. "Whatever, man." I turn and walk back across the room to my locker to finish getting dressed. Corey jeers behind me, but I block him out and get into my pregame headspace.

I'm still thinking about what Corey said in the first period and I lay a pretty nasty check on a guy and nearly get called for boarding. It was a clean hit.. mostly. I could have been a little less aggressive because he wasn't even anywhere near the play, but I'm pissed off.

I knew that switching teams would be hard. The new guys are always outsiders for a bit, and they take a lot of ribbing in the beginning, as a hazing of sorts. But Corey's attack felt more personal than just the normal teasing and mild pranks.

Does the rest of the team feel the same way about me? Do they think I'm just a bunny-fucking playboy?

If that's what they think, then fuck them. I know the truth. I know that isn't how I do things anymore.

I know that what Brenna and I have is real.

I can see her in the stands from the bench, her long hair in soft waves cradling her face. She's wearing my jersey again and I have to keep ignoring that fact because it's such a goddamn turn-on. She's been watching the game closely, occasionally leaning over to talk with Patrick's mom and sister. The seat next to Brenna is still empty, and that's how it will remain.

From the bench, I watch Patrick lead the charge up the middle. Just past the blue line, he dekes to the right and fires off a shot, sailing past the opposing team's goalie and into the net. Instantly the whole team is on our feet, celebrating and congratulating Patrick on a great goal.

"Fucker makes it look easy," Nils says from next to me, his accent thick.

"No shit," I say back. Patrick skates past the bench, accepting gloved high fives as congratulations from each of us down the line.

I'm itching to get back onto the ice, but Coach has kept me to minimal ice time this game. I'm hoping it's to give some of the prospects a chance to try for spots in the big times because I'm already a sure thing, but I'm not 100% confident in that assumption.

Late into the third period, we're tied with the St. Louis Trackers 2-2. My skating has been solid tonight but the defense has been equally as solid, so I haven't had any good opportunities in my limited playing time.

I hop the boards with less than two minutes left in the period, charging hard toward the opposing net. Patrick clears the puck over the blue line before I get to it and I head to the right side as he dumps it in, the puck circling around behind the net and along the boards. I meet the puck at the side, slamming on the brakes and avoiding a check by one of their defensemen. I poke the puck out from between the guy's feet and Nils finds it. He slaps it back to one of the young defensemen who is waiting at the top of the circle. As Nils does that, I go to cut through the middle. The kid doesn't miss as he whacks the puck into the slot where it connects with the blade of my stick. Like lightning, I flick the puck up and over the goalie's shoulder and into the net.

The euphoria of scoring a goal never gets old.

Patrick, Nils, the young kid on defense and Matus all swarm me with congratulatory helmet slaps and high fives as the sound of the horn blaring, announcing the goal to the arena, fills my ears. We skate along the bench and I get glove taps from the rest of the team.

Then my eyes find Brenna in the stands, where she is jumping and cheering like we won the fucking Stanley Cup.

God, I think I love this girl.

No, I can't. Ryan Flynn doesn't fall in love. Especially not after just a few short weeks. I hop back onto the bench and try to get focused back on the game. After all, we have to hold onto our lead for another 47 seconds to win the game.

But as sweet as it is to score my first goal with my new team, it's sweeter watching my girl cheering me on in the stands.

The girl I'm in love with.

…Shit.

21. BRENNA

I'm at work on Monday, knee deep in a project with Natalie. It's a huge opportunity for our company to be presenting at an international conference, so our materials need to be perfect.

Of course, Natalie takes every opportunity possible to ask me about Ryan. She is still completely clueless when it comes to hockey, but it's kind of adorable how she has started reading the headlines for his games to have a way to bring the team – and him – up in conversation.

I'm poring over the "swag" for the conference – which is the ridiculous yet widely accepted name in the marketing industry for giveaway items to promote a business. Currently, I'm reviewing a sample print of our new brochures for the conference, looking for any uneven borders or typos, with Natalie sitting across the desk from me, staring at a large poster that arrived today. It'll be displayed at the booth, alongside a couple other posters I designed as well as several videos that Natalie made. It's so neat to be able to see my work in print rather than just on a computer screen like I normally see it.

"So I saw that your boy got a goal in the game last night!" Natalie says suddenly, breaking the silence. "It is called a goal, right?"

I laugh as I flip over the brochure to look at the back. Apparently he knows even less about hockey than I do. "Yes Nat, he scored a goal. Technically, it was the game-winning goal."

"That's so awesome!" She says excitedly. Then, she lowers her voice, "Does that mean he scored in bed last night too?"

"Oh my god, I'm not answering that," I say, my cheeks flushing.

"Well, you just gave me my answer," she says, her red lips quirking into a smirk. I throw the pamphlet at her and it floats harmlessly to the floor.

A knock at the door startles both of us. We had purposely shut ourselves in my office this morning and put our phones on Do Not Disturb, with explicit instructions given to the administrative assistant to not disturb us, so I'm a little irritated when she opens the door. "Brenna, I know you're not taking calls, but... it's Ryan, and he's called a few times already today."

"I guess that's a worthy interruption, then," Natalie says, smiling at me. I've already got the phone receiver in my hand and am picking up his call off of park before the administrative assistant has even closed the door.

"Ryan?"

"Brenna!" He says. His voice always fills me with warmth. "I'm sorry to interrupt you – I know today is a super busy day for you but everything's okay."

I let out a small sigh of relief. "You had me worried something happened to you at practice."

"I'm sorry, I didn't mean to worry you," he says, and he sounds really deflated.

"It's okay! I should have told the receptionist to hold all calls except yours. Anyway, what did you need to talk to me about?"

"Don't go home after work today. I need you to meet me somewhere." He gives me the address to a place called Sixteen. I haven't heard of it, but I'm learning not to question Ryan and just go with his plan.

After Ryan and I have hung up, Natalie is facing me, her smile eight miles wide. "He's taking you to *Sixteen*?" she squeals.

I tuck a strand of hair back behind my ear again as I pick up the box of bright green pens with our company logo on them from the other side of the desk and set them in front of me. "I'm assuming you know what Sixteen is?"

"Brenna. Sixteen is an extremely nice restaurant in Trump Tower." Natalie leans back in her chair, biting her thumbnail thoughtfully as she stares off into the distance. "Your boy sure knows how to treat a girl right."

I look down at my outfit and frown. "Uh, Nat? I don't think I'm going to Sixteen. They won't let me in the door if I show up in this." I knew today would be rough, so I wore one of my loose and somewhat tattered dresses. It's passable in the office but absolutely not at a fancy restaurant.

As if on cue, there's another knock on the door and the administrative assistant appears with several shopping bags in her hands. I recognize some of the designer names from having walked by their stores on the Magnificent Mile, but that's all I'd ever done – walked by. I would never be able to afford anything from any of those stores. "Ryan said you may need these."

Twenty minutes later, Natalie and I have unloaded and laid out sixteen different outfits. I catch and appreciate his wit in buying me the same number of outfits as the name of the place he's taking me, but it's a little overwhelming. These aren't just dressy outfits - these are all formal, designer pieces, in a variety of cuts, fabrics and colors. I was starting to grow accustomed to Ryan's gift-giving habit, but this is to the extreme.

I feel a panic starting to rise up in me as I look over the dresses, but Natalie's arm around me comforts me.

"Just breathe, pick one, and don't think about it," she says to me. "Just go, and be."

The Uber drops me off in front of Trump Tower and I stand on the sidewalk for a moment, smoothing out the bottom of the red peplum dress from St. John that I ended up choosing for tonight out of the options Ryan had given me.

I step into the lobby, taking in the lavish décor, and follow the signs to an elevator leading to Sixteen. Fittingly, it's on the 16th floor of the building, and before I know it, the elevator doors slide open and I step out into an elegant marble foyer.

Ryan is standing in the center of the room, greeting me with his thousand watt smile and a black tuxedo. His hair is freshly cut, his beard neatly groomed and his shoes polished to an impeccable shine.

"Hey," I say softly, my cheeks flushing as he gazes appreciatively over me. I'm also gazing appreciatively over him, so I don't mind.

"You look... indescribable," he says. He captures the side of my face with his hand and my mouth with his. The kiss is all heat and passion, but we pull apart abruptly when someone clears their throat.

"Mr. Flynn, your table is ready," the waiter says to Ryan, gesturing through a hallway lined with hundreds upon hundreds of wine bottles, and across the dining room to the 30 foot floor-to-ceiling windows spanning one entire curved wall. It's at this point that I realize we are the only patrons in the entire restaurant.

Ryan takes my hand as the waiter leads us through the maze of empty tables and chairs. "Where is everyone?" I ask him.

"I rented out the restaurant for us tonight." Ryan says this so nonchalantly, like it's the most normal thing in the world.

"Y-You what?" I stammer, stumbling in the pair of Jimmy Choos that match the dress perfectly. Ryan pulls out a chair from a table next to the giant glass windows and I clumsily slide into it. He takes a seat across the table from me.

"I wanted to do something special tonight. Something spontaneous." He chuckles. "Well, spontaneous for you. It took quite a bit of planning on my side to make this all happen. But it's worth it for you."

The waiter disappears as the Sommelier pours a very expensive looking wine into our glasses. I stare at Ryan, dumbstruck. "Ryan... this is just too much."

"Nothing could ever be too much when it comes to you, Brenna," he says, reaching across the table and taking one of my delicate hands in his calloused one. It's an ironic and backwards reflection of our lives as a whole – the same, yet so incredibly different.

"You don't think sixteen outfits is excessive? Or renting out an entire restaurant just for us?"

"No, I don't," he says with a tone of finality. "Brenna, I lov--" His eyes are searching mine, and I know he's just realized what he's about to say, and that I might run away from him again. He clears his throat and tries again. "Brenna, I like you... a lot."

I take a deep breath to ground myself. "Okay. I think I'll be okay. It's just…" I release my hand from his and use it to gesture around the room. "All this? It's a lot for a girl like me to take in. I could never afford to eat here even once on my own, let alone rent out the whole damn restaurant for a night. And the outfits too?" I take another breath to quell the panic threatening to bubble up out of me. Apparently I'm not as okay as I thought I was a few seconds ago. "Your lifestyle is *so* different from mine. It's flattering and so completely overwhelming."

I instantly regret the hurt in his eyes that my shortcomings are responsible for causing. "I'm sorry for freaking you out," he says softly. "You know I love to give gifts, but I can see how it would overwhelm you. God, I'm such an idiot."

"No, it's okay!" I quickly stammer out, taking his hand in mine again. "I understand why you're doing it. It's just the *level* of it, that's all. I mean, every girl loves getting presents. But Ashton never bought me a single thing, so you've got to understand that going from zero to six million is leaving me with a little whiplash."

Ryan laughs that delectable, full-bodied sound that I've come to love, and I smile, the tension and anxiety loosening their grip on both of us.

"We can go home, if you want," he says softly. "Pretend this disaster never happened."

I shake my head. "No. You put so much effort into doing something amazing for me. We're staying." Ryan has the biggest heart of anyone I've ever met. I am determined to enjoy this, to be okay and not let my anxiety eat me alive for once. His smile makes me feel like it is something I can achieve.

22. RYAN

After an exquisite eight course meal that my trainer will definitely kill me for, Brenna and I head out onto the rooftop terrace overlooking downtown. We stand silently at the edge, Chicago alive with light and sound even in the oncoming autumn dusk. The river flows quietly past us and into Lake Michigan in the distance.

Being able to enjoy this city, and these simple moments with the person who brings me so much joy, means more to me than anyone knows. I feel a level of peace and calm that I don't think I've ever experienced in my life, especially not since Sam died. Everything was turbulence before I met Brenna in the bar that night.

She reigns me in, keeps me calm.

But she also drives me wild.

She shivers against the cool breeze, the last few tendrils of sunlight stretching themselves through her hair and across her skin. I wrap my arms around her, capturing her body against mine. Every soft curve of her fits perfectly into my own spaces.

I kiss her long and slow, savoring the exotic taste and feel of her lips on mine. Our tongues dance together, erasing all thoughts from my mind. I can only breathe, and feel, and love.

I lead her to one of the outdoor sofas in the middle of the terrace and decide that tonight, I'm not going to tell her, but rather show her that I love her.

For the first time in my life, I don't have sex with a woman - I make love to her.

23. BRENNA

The next couple weeks go by quickly. Ryan has several away games, and I begin to get a feel for what it will be like during the regular season when he's traveling constantly. Thankfully, I've been spending a lot of time with Morgan. She's fun and quirky, and her hockey knowledge is extensive, to say the least. She's been helping keep me sane when Ryan is away.

I drop by the bar where Morgan works Friday evening after I get off work. The Velocity are playing in New York tonight so we decided that I would stop by and watch the game at the bar while she works. It's only a couple blocks from the arena so I find it easily.

The bar is surprisingly large on the inside, with a small-town coffee-shop vibe. Strings of lights hang across the ceiling. The walls are covered in an eclectic mix of local art and chalkboard paint, and the large, mismatched sofas and chairs scattered around the place feel warm and inviting.

"Over here, Brenna!" Morgan waves at me from across the room. She has the remote in her other hand, in the middle of switching the channel on the tv closest to the bar.

I plop onto one of the stools. "Has it started yet?"
"Nope, you're just in time!" She says. She's wearing a faded Velocity shirt and high-waisted jeans paired with black ankle boots. "New York has been really good so far in preseason so this is gonna be a tough one for the boys."

"Better start drinking now, then!" I say with a laugh. Morgan pours me a beer and slides it across the bar to me. Thankfully, the place is fairly empty, with only a handful of college students studying in the back corner, and a young couple munching on a basket of fries near the front window, so Morgan is able to relax and watch the game with me for the most part.

"So things are getting pretty serious with you and Flynn, huh?" she asks me, using the common sports-life practice of referring to someone by their last name. She props her elbows on the edge of the bar top and rests her chin in her hands.

I run the tip of my finger across the glass of beer, collecting the condensation on my skin. "I suppose you could say that." Two bouquets of flowers, a Velocity t-shirt and a Victoria's Secret gift card were all delivered to me... just this week. We have been video chatting every single night and texting at every free moment.

147

I didn't think I'd miss him this much, but I do.

"How are you handling the increased media attention?"

"You are just going straight for the tough questions, huh?" I say, lifting the beer to my lips and taking a long drink from it. I set it back down into the circle of liquid left on the bar top. "I mean, it's all still very overwhelming. We're trying to lay low since our relationship is still so new. I'm also trying to not be a distraction from him making the team. I know he'd hate to be sent down to the minors."

Morgan glances at the tv, where the puck has just been dropped, and then refocuses her attention on me. "What does your family think of him?"

I clear my throat. "Well, I don't associate with my family anymore, so, even if they somehow know, their opinions don't matter."

"Shit, I'm sorry," Morgan reaches out and touches my hand. "I didn't know."

"It's okay," I say, taking another drink from my glass. It's already half-empty. "Nobody really knows about that part of my life… not even Ryan."

As if he knew we were talking about him, I see him check a New York player into the boards. It's a solid hit and New York isn't happy about it. One of their players immediately skates to Ryan and takes a couple swings at him, but they are quickly pulled apart by the officials.

"Your boy is awfully scrappy tonight," Morgan muses.

"He's got something to prove," I say softly. Although we haven't talked about it, I know his father's unexpected visit a few weeks ago threw Ryan for a loop and he's still reeling from it. It's part of why I haven't brought up the subject of my parents - because I know Ryan doesn't want to talk about his, just as much as I don't want to talk about mine.

I still wonder about that photo I saw in his house that one morning. Sam Flynn. Why has Ryan never mentioned having a brother? Is it for the same reason I don't talk about having a step-sister?

As if on cue, my phone buzzes in my pocket. I see the phone number I could never lose from my memory, and the message "I'm in town tonight, would love to see you and talk." Fuck. Me.

I lay my phone face-down on the bar top, ignoring Morgan's slightly bemused expression. I down the rest of my beer in one go, and slide the glass across the wooden bar to Morgan. "I'm going to need something stronger."

I am simultaneously feeling pretty good and pretty bad by the time the third period rolls around. I'm sporting a hefty buzz because I switched to drinking vodka cranberry and Morgan is pouring them strong.

The Velocity are losing 4-1 in a pretty brutal game. New York is making them look like a pee wee team tonight. I know the phrase "you win some, you lose some," but this will be their first loss in pre-season this year, which sucks since it's also their last pre-season game.

My phone has also gone off with several more text messages that I am ignoring. Morgan raises an eyebrow at me each time one comes through when I don't move to check them. To her credit, she hasn't probed, but I can tell it's killing her not to ask.

Toward the end of the third period, I feel a tap on my shoulder. Confused, I spin around in my chair, and come face-to-face with none other than the guy who damn near ruined my life: Ashton.

"Hey B!" He says to me, his straight, shaggy brown hair longer than I remember it being, falling in front of his steel colored eyes. He tries to hug me and since I'm sitting on a stool at the bar, I can't dodge him, so I'm trapped. He wraps his arms around me and I stare wide-eyed at Morgan, who understandably looks confused as hell.

"Ashton," I say sharply, pulling away from the embrace as quickly as possible. "What are you doing here?"

"Didn't you get my texts? I'm in town tonight and I needed to see my favorite girl."

My head is spinning. Morgan clears her throat and thrusts her hand out to shake Ashton's. "Hey, I'm Morgan, Brenna's friend. Can I get you something to drink?"

"Nice to meet you, Morgan," Ashton says, throwing her one of his patented, charming smiles. "Jack and Coke, doll."

Morgan goes to make his drink, glancing back at me for a moment. Making sure I'm okay? I'm not okay but I can't exactly vocalize that, even if I wanted to. Ashton gazes appreciatively at her ass for a moment before turning back to me.

"How did you even find me?" I ask him. He's standing too close to me and I feel claustrophobic.

"It wasn't hard, B," he laughs. "You weren't responding to my texts, so I texted Carly. What are you doing at this place anyway? It's kind of a dive, don't you think?"

Morgan sets Ashton's glass on the bar in front of us with a loud thunk. I'm pissed. Why would Carly tell Ashton where I am? She calls him Fuckface, for gods sake.

Fuck Carly for putting me in this situation. Our friendship is over.

"Aren't you excited that I'm here?" Ashton asks me.

I finally look him in the eye for the first time since he arrived. I feel anger, excitement, and those familiar butterflies that have plagued me for nearly a decade. "I don't know what to feel," I answer him honestly.

I vaguely hear the horn on the tv and glance up to see that the Velocity lost 5-1 tonight. Morgan is not even trying to hide the fact that she's staring at us both. I look back at Ashton. "Did you forget how things went down the last time I saw you?"

"Of course not, B," he says, taking a large gulp from his drink. "But since some time has passed, and I'm sure you've missed me, I figured tonight we could see each other since we're both thinking more rationally."

"Rationally!?" I nearly yell. "How could I be rational after what you did?"

"B, baby," Ashton shushes me. If anyone else tried to do that to me, I'd go postal - but I immediately quiet at Ashton's voice. "Come on, let's get out of here. Let's go somewhere and talk."

I look at Morgan. She's concerned and confused. Me too, girl.

Without a doubt, I shouldn't go. I absolutely can't trust Ashton farther than I can throw him. But part of me wants to hear him out, and maybe get some closure to that chapter of my life.

Deciding to give him the benefit of the doubt, I sigh. "Okay, let's go."

24. RYAN

Brenna won't answer her fucking phone.

It's 3am in New York and I'm on a fucking red eye flight back to Chicago. I bought the ticket after she wouldn't answer any of my calls or texts for two hours straight.

I'm not sure if I'm more confused or pissed off.

We lost a brutal game tonight against the New York Pirates and I needed to hear my girl's voice. Tonight was my last chance to prove to the management team that I deserve a spot on the Velocity's roster this season. I hope I earned my spot but I'm really not sure. Brenna calms me down, reassures me that I deserve to be here in the NHL. I need her tonight and she isn't fucking answering me.

After two hours, I finally called Carly. She let me know that she didn't know where Brenna was and she was trying to find her too. Carly then told me that Morgan had texted her saying that Brenna had left the bar with Ashton. Although I don't know Carly all that well, the terror in her voice was all I needed to hop on the next flight home.

Brenna has been light on the details regarding her douchebag ex-boyfriend, but I know enough to know this guy is bad news. He's narcissistic, manipulative and whatever he did to Brenna really fucked her up. I still have to remind her every day that she's beautiful, thoughtful, talented, and perfect.

Why would she go somewhere with him, alone? Why would she not tell her friends where she was going? And why would she completely blow me off when we talk for hours after every single game?

Am I more committed to her than she is to me?

The plane can't get to the Windy City fast enough.

25. BRENNA

I've been walking for so many miles tonight that my feet are going to hurt for days, I'm sure.

But nothing hurts as badly as my heart does.

Ashton and I have been walking the streets of Chicago for several hours, talking about anything and everything. Conversation has always been natural for us, so once he broke through my guard, it's been flowing steadily, like the old days. He's asked questions about me and my life, what I've been up to for the past year, if I still frequent that breakfast place over on Cicero, how Carly is doing...

Ashton never gave a shit about me, my interests, or my friends. Who is this guy and where did he come from?

Okay, I can't say he *never* cared. For brief times here and there, he did. Whether he was faking it or not, I can't say for sure, but there were times where he was caring, supportive, and sweet. He was a real, loving boyfriend for a while. When times were good, they were *good*. Those good times cover the memories of the bad times with him.

Maybe I'm an idealist, but I always try to see the best in everyone – even Ashton. So when he asked me to go for a walk, I figured it couldn't hurt. Maybe he's changed, and I should give him the opportunity to tell his side of the story. I would hope he would afford me the same opportunity if the roles were reversed.

I feel tingly with a mix of booze, butterflies, and the familiarity of two souls that know each other so intimately. My legs fall into stride with his as we walk, naturally, like it hasn't been a full trip around the sun since they last lined up with each other.

We stop in front of the iconic Willis Tower, the glass façade glittering against the sky with the reflection of city lights in the cool night air.

"Remember the first night we went for a walk?" Ashton asks me suddenly. "We tried to walk all the way here from campus."

"Yeah. You said it would be a good workout. But neither of us realized it would have been 14 miles one way to get here," I say with a laugh. Ashton's laugh is familiar.. comforting. He's very close to me again.

He takes one of my hands in his, sliding his thumb across mine. "What happened to us, B?"

My guard shoots back up and I take a step back from him, breaking the connection but not fully escaping his spell. "Ashton, you cheated on me. *You* tell *me* what happened to us."

"B, baby," Ashton grabs my hand again. I half-heartedly try to pull it from his grip, but quickly give up, focused instead on his touch. "I was young and stupid. I realize that now. I want to clear the air between us... I want to make things right."

"So you aren't engaged to her anymore?"

"No," he says, a bit of something to his voice... sadness, maybe? "All I can think about is you. Every minute of every goddamn day. You've always been my girl, B. You'll always be my girl."

My heart stops.

He is holding both of my hands now, between us. All I can feel is the sensation of his thumbs rubbing my skin, and the fire in my lungs from the breath I've been holding.

A few people walk past, but they ignore us. "I know I hurt you more than I could ever understand but I know what a huge mistake I made, and I want to make it right. No one else will have my heart, B... only you."

"Ashton, I-"

The words die on my lips as Ashton's mouth seals over mine. Any anger, any resolve I still had, die with those words as I sink into the comfortable numbness of his kiss. I may have consciously forgotten the minor details of him, but our mouths certainly did not forget each other. My mind is blank, caught in suspension.

Then I see Ryan's face in my mind.

I jerk away from Ashton, needing complete separation.

"What's the matter, B?"

"Ashton, I have a boyfriend," I stammer. "I'm seeing someone." My hands are shaking.

"You what!?" Ashton yells. His voice bounces off the steel and glass edifices surrounding us. I cringe, bracing myself for the verbal assault I'm about to endure. "How dare you, Brenna? How can you be seeing someone?"

"You *left* me!"

"But you told me that I would be yours – forever. I thought forever meant something to you. Did you lie to me?" He's inches from my face. Even in the night, I can see the rage in his eyes.

"No, but-"

"I came back for you, Brenna. I fucking came back here when I realized what a mistake I had made. And this is what I come back to - you fucking another guy? Who is this fucker?"

"Please calm down," I beg him. One passerby looks our way but doesn't stop. Typical Chicago.

"You know, you're a real piece of work," Ashton snarls at me. "This guy better run while he still can. You're just going to destroy him too, like you do everything else. He won't want you much longer. You're a worthless piece of shit."

Shaking, I try to speak, but he cuts me off before I can get any words out. "You really think you're worthy of love? You think someone could love someone like you? You're messed up, Brenna. This guy will leave you like everyone else, and don't you dare come crawling back to me."

I'm sobbing openly in the streets of downtown Chicago in the middle of the night and I don't even care. "Ashton, I'm sorry-" I'm reaching out for him, but he starts backing away from me.

"You go back to that happy little world inside your head. Keep believing that you're a "hero," that you're actually making a difference in the world. You're nothing but fucking trailer trash and you're never going to amount to anything. I'm done with you, Brenna."

His back is to me and he's walking away from me once again. I sink to the concrete which rumbles beneath me, the city never sleeping, even at this ungodly hour.

I thought I had already been broken a year ago when I found out he was cheating on me. I broke even more when when I found out he was engaged to the girl with whom he was cheating on me. I believed I had been broken as much as any one single person could be when I discovered the girl he was cheating on me with and now engaged to was my own step-sister.

Somehow, this is even worse.

I don't know how Ashton always manages to get me under his spell. I know better than to fall for his old tricks but... somehow I always get dragged back in. The timbre of his voice, the sensation of his touch, it all lulls me into complacency before he destroys me again.

The power he has over me, even to this day, blows me away.

And now I'm questioning everything.

I lay back, my shoulder blades scraping the concrete sidewalk, and sob to the sky.

26. RYAN

I search all night for Brenna, driving all over her neighborhood, the area around the bar and arena, and even scoping out Northwestern's campuses. I call her phone no less than 300 times. I want to get the police involved, but Carly won't let me, convincing me that although Ashton is scary, he isn't the type to kidnap and hurt my girl.

At least, not physically, she said.

Between myself, Carly, John and Morgan, we piece together that Ashton showed up at the bar, claiming that Carly had told him that's where Brenna was. However, Carly never spoke to Ashton. According to Carly, Ashton has tracked her cell phone before and then lied about how he knew where she was.

Carly also fills Morgan and I in on some of Brenna and Ashton's history. Specifically, how last year, Brenna discovered Ashton was engaged to Brenna's step-sister, Jenny, while he was still dating Brenna. When everything blew up, Brenna's dad sided with Jenny, telling Brenna to her face that "Ashton would have proposed to you already if he was really interested in you." No wonder Brenna doesn't talk about anyone in her family, ever. I guess I probably wouldn't either if my ex-boyfriend was cheating on me with my step-sister for who even knows how long, to the point of proposing to her and moving with her to Texas.

At 10am, I park my car down the block from Carly and Brenna's house. I've been awake for more than 24 hours at this point, and I had played a hockey game in New York before driving the entire city of Chicago through the wee hours of the morning. I've started to fade fast, and I know it isn't safe for me to keep driving at this point. I decide to take a quick cat nap in my car, then reconnect with Carly to see if we need to get the police involved.

I close my eyes for only a few moments before someone starts knocking on the window of my car. Frustrated, I open my eyes, and bolt upright when I see that it's Morgan. I roll down the window. "Brenna just called Carly. She's okay."

I quickly jump out of my car, not even bothering to roll the window back up. "Where is she?" I'm walking down the block toward the house so quickly that Morgan has to nearly run to keep up with my steps.

"We don't know. She wouldn't say."

The door of the house flings open before I even reach it and I see John there, looking worn out but relieved. I push past him and find Carly standing in the kitchen, staring at her phone.

"Where is she?" I ask her before I even reach her.

"She won't tell me," she sighs. "She said she's okay, but she wants to be alone right now."

A flash of white-hot anger tears through me. "I don't know what that fucker did to her but I will kick his ass."

John puts his hand on my shoulder, temporarily grounding me. "She also told Carly that she needs space... from you, Ryan."

I spin around to face John. Morgan is standing behind him. "From me? Why?"

"We don't know," he says.

"Well, I hate to be the bearer of bad news, but I think I know why," Morgan says from behind me. We all turn to her and she's holding out her phone. On the screen are three photos. The first is Brenna at Two Bits, with a guy standing behind her. It must be Ashton, because the next photo is the two of them crossing the street.

The third photo is Brenna and Ashton, lips locked, in front of the Willis Tower.

The rock in my stomach drops through the floor.

Carly cuts the silence with a defeated sigh. "Brenna didn't tell me much except that she wants to come home, but she won't if Ryan is here."

"I don't understand any of this," I say, looking at each of them for answers. "What the hell is going on?"

"Brenna is... she's different than most," says Carly. "I think she needs to process whatever happened tonight, and handle it in her own Brenna way. She'll come around, Ryan. She always does, eventually. She just needs time."

My throat is tight. "I guess I don't really have much of a choice then, do I?" A stale laugh dies on my lips. "I'm going to go." John and Morgan move out of the way so I can get past them to the front door. I pause before I pull it open, and look over my shoulder, and say softly, "Please tell Brenna that I love her... no matter what, I still love her."

I close the door behind me.

27. BRENNA

One month later

The night Ashton left me standing alone in the streets of downtown Chicago in the middle of the night, I was at my lowest point. Broken, I wandered the streets for several hours, letting my mind run – and run it did. I questioned everything about myself, my life, my goals, my friends, my relationships. All of it was up for questioning, consideration, and self-destruction.

My heart was shattered. Around 4am, I ended up on top of the double-decker bridge on North Wells Street connecting The Loop to River North. The bottom of the bridge is for cars and pedestrians, and the top is for the L, Chicago's train system. It's one of those draw bridges that is split in the center and lifts up on each side to let big boats down the Chicago River. I climbed to the top of the impressive structure and walked along the tracks to the middle of the bridge. There, I sat on the edge, staring into the dark waters of the Chicago River moving beneath me from the famous reddish-orange trusses.

If I would have jumped, it wouldn't have been a far enough fall to kill me.

Even if it had, it wouldn't have solved anything. Ashton would have gotten away with what he's done to me over all these years, and I would have left a lot of people behind.

Carly, John, Morgan, even Natalie...

And Ryan.

I eventually climbed down and wandered the streets, from River North to the Streeterville neighborhood and along the shore of Lake Michigan as the sun rose over the lake. I walked all the way to Lincoln Park. It took hours and my feet became giant, bloody blisters in my old Toms, but I was too broken to care.

Sitting on a bench at the edge of the giant lake, watching the morning sunlight reflecting off the waves, I realized that I couldn't let this destroy me. The night had ended and the sun rose again. I needed to do the same.

By the time I finally came out of my stupor, it was almost 10am. My phone had been dead for hours, so I bought a charger from a 24-hour convenience store and plugged it in at Starbucks. When it turned on, I had so many missed calls, texts and voicemails that it actually crashed my phone. After a couple restarts, I was finally able to call Carly and let her know I'd be home soon.

When the Uber dropped me off an hour later, John, Carly, and Morgan all met me at the door. Their concern and love filled my heart and helped mend some of the damage I had taken that night.

But I couldn't face Ryan. I was afraid of what I'd say to him, but even more afraid of what he'd say to me.

I was sure Carly had filled him in at least a little of my history with Ashton, but I could only imagine what was going through his head when he found out his girlfriend had left the bar with her manipulative ex-boyfriend and then no one heard from her for twelve hours except for the paparazzi photos that ended up online of us kissing.

Apparently Ryan had even jumped on a plane to come to Chicago after his game when he got the call that I was missing. I'm sure it was expensive, and made him look bad to the team, and he probably got no sleep because he was worrying about me.

Stupid. I was so, so stupid to trust Ashton. I was foolish to even entertain the idea that I could receive answers or closure from him that night. I put myself into a bad situation, and I have to deal with the consequences of my actions.

Through therapy, I've been learning that loving myself is most important, and loving others needs to be second. I've always put myself last and everyone else first, so now I am making an active effort to choose myself and my happiness over others. It's been a journey, but I'm learning to love who I am.

And who I am loves Ryan Flynn.

I just hope that, after everything I've put him through, he could still love me back.

I'm getting ready to go to the Velocity's home game with Morgan tonight. Since I haven't spoken to Ryan in over a month, I can't exactly ask him if I can use one of his tickets, so Theresa gladly gave up her seat for me. I debate on if I should wear his jersey since we aren't together, and almost decide not to, but end up throwing it on at the last second. Wearing a jersey with his name and number on it makes me happy.

Morgan picks me up and we head to the arena. She's chattering away as she drives, and I'm absently scrolling on my phone when suddenly, a message comes through from Carly. I click the link she's sent and my phone pulls up one of the hockey blogs I've seen before.

The headline reads: *Ryan Flynn's Biggest Secret – And It Isn't His Cheating Girlfriend!*

I read it off to Morgan. "Oh man," she says. "You have to read the entire thing out loud."

I take a deep breath, and begin reading.

Normally I brush off "information" that comes from anonymous sources, however this one is too interesting to not address.

I received an email a couple weeks ago from an anonymous tipster stating
they had information on Ryan Flynn's notoriously private personal life.
Intrigued, I emailed back, and boy oh boy, did this source provide!
According to this tipster, NHL playboy Ryan Flynn had an older brother.
Yes, you read that right. Two Flynn boys! Apparently this older Flynn boy
was quite the skater and would have likely been an NHL star just like his
little bro. Unfortunately, Samuel Flynn passed away in 2003, when he was
only 16 years old. Ryan would have been 12 at that time.
I did some digging into the legitimacy of this claim. It took a bit of work,
but sure enough, I was able to procure the obituary information for Samuel
John Flynn.

The article then has a scanned image of an obituary from a
newspaper. It's very straightforward, simply stating that Sam
passed away unexpectedly, his surviving family, and the date and
time of his memorial service.

While looking for information on Samuel Flynn, I also turned up something
else very interesting from Ryan's mysterious past: An obituary for his
mother, Daisy Flynn, from five years ago, who died of a heart attack.
I wonder why Ryan never mentions his dead brother or mother? Shame?
Grief? Or something more?
So there you have it, a bad boy with a mysterious past. Thanks to "A" for
the tip on this one!

Morgan and I are both silent for several seconds, absorbing
what we've just learned.

"Did you know..." she begins to ask me, trailing off.

"No. I mean, not exactly," I say. "I was, um, snooping one time, and I found a photo of him and Sam. I never had the right opportunity to ask him about it. He's never mentioned having a brother, or that his mom is dead."

"Holy shit, dude," she says. I nod in agreement. As if me showing up at his game wouldn't be enough of a surprise, this information hitting the news is the topping on a shit-cake.

Even worse, I know it was Ashton who sent in the info to that blog site. I haven't been avoiding just Ryan, but also Ashton. It didn't take much work for Ashton to figure out who my boyfriend was, and he's been texting me non-stop ever since, calling me every degrading word in the dictionary. At the strong recommendation of Jane, I finally blocked his number for some reprieve. This must be his way to get to me… and Ryan.

28. RYAN

I'm just arriving at the arena when my phone starts to ring. I throw my bag down on the bench and pull my phone out of my pocket, and see that the caller is my father.

"Hello?" I answer, confused as to why he'd be calling me.

"Someone leaked to the press about your mother and Sam and now all the sports networks are calling here non-stop. Who the fuck did you tell?"

My heart stops. "I didn't tell anyone!"

"How the hell did some website find out then?" He's slurring his words slightly, as usual.

"I don't know, father" I run my free hand through my hair. This is *not* how I wanted this game day to go.

He hangs up suddenly, probably off to drain another fifth and complain to the walls about me. I pace the locker room quickly, knowing that the rest of the team will start arriving any minute but needing to walk out some of the stress that just spiked inside me.

I launch into my regular pre-game routine, resolving to deal with it all after the game. There's nothing I can do about any of it right now anyway.

I glide out onto the ice to begin warmups. As is my normal pre-game ritual, I skate once around the entire arena before allowing myself to look up at my reserved seats – both sitting empty for my mother and brother who never had the chance to see me play in the NHL and never will.

However when I look up into the stands tonight, I lock eyes with Brenna, who is sitting with Morgan next to my two empty seats. She gives me a shy smile and a small wave. My heart skips a beat and I nearly miss my next step. Nils pokes me in the back with his stick.

"Quit daydreaming, Flynn," he laughs.

"Shut it, Larsson," I poke him back.

I haven't seen Brenna in weeks. It's been radio silence since the night Ashton showed up in town. I gave her a week to process before I started trying to get in touch with her. At first, my messages were very top-level concern. When she didn't respond, I began getting angry. I'd leave a voicemail yelling at her, and then immediately call back and apologize. After a while, Carly finally called me and told me to stop trying to talk to her. It was the wake up call I needed.

So I walked away.

Now she's here to watch my game. Is she here to watch me specifically, or just to hang out with Morgan? I fire one of the practice pucks into the net and skate around the back to the other side. I don't know what to think or how to feel. All I know is that the last four weeks without this woman in my life have been some of the longest, worst weeks of my entire life. I have been having to force myself to eat and I've barely slept at all. There have been opportunities to fuck a few puck bunnies while on the road but I haven't even left the hotel room on our road game trips other than for the games themselves because all I can think about is Brenna.

I miss her beyond words.

I have to get through this game.

We manage to scrape out a win, no thanks to me. I played like shit but I don't even care. I need to do damage control on the family situation, but first, I need to see Brenna.

She's waiting in the family waiting area when I come out of the locker room after the game. It's as if I'm seeing her for the very first time. Her blonde hair falls in waves over her shoulders, longer than I remember. She looks healthy, strong, confident. She's wearing my jersey and my mind flashes back to the time she sucked my dick while wearing it. I push the memory out of my mind.

"Hey Brenna," I say, my guard up.

"Hey Ryan," she says softly. Her dark eyes search my face, tracking across me before settling on my mouth. I feel a smile pull at my lips.

"Can we go talk somewhere?" I ask her. She nods. "We'll go out the back. I'd rather not face any of the reporters right now."

"You know about the article?" she asks, gathering her purse and coat from the chair next to Morgan.

I wave bye to Morgan and head for the back door. "Yeah... That's part of what I need to talk to you about."

We head out into the night. The late October air has finally lost all traces of residual summer warmth, and Brenna pulls her jacket around herself a little tighter in the chilly breeze. I hold the car door open for her, shutting it once she's seated and head around the back of the car to get in.

Once we are on the road headed toward my house, Brenna starts to speak. "Ryan, I need to apologize to you for what happened last month. I am so sorry for so many things, and it's taken me a while to forgive myself so that I'd be able to ask you for forgiveness as well." She takes a deep breath and lets it out slowly. "I'm sorry for disappearing with Ashton that night. It was a bad decision for me to leave with him at all, but to do it and not keep anyone in the loop was irresponsible."

The skyline begins to disappear into the distance behind us as she continues. "I'm sorry for falling for his mind tricks again. I don't know how or why, but I have always allowed Ashton to have this grip on my emotions and my life. My therapist is helping me to unravel his hold on me and move on from everything."

"Your therapist?" I ask her, sneaking a glance in her direction before changing lanes.

"Yes. I started seeing Jane right after everything happened. She's been really great. I've always thought that I could face my struggles on my own, but Jane has been helping me learn that you can't always tackle everything on your own, and that it's okay to ask for help."

"That's so great, Brenna," I tell her honestly. "I'm proud of you for taking steps to help yourself."

I see her smile out of the corner of my eye, her face illuminated in the street lights as we exit the freeway onto the smaller streets of the suburbs. "Thank you. It's been hard to open up to someone and come to terms with everything I've been through, especially with Ashton, but I can already tell it's paying off for me." She clears her throat before taking a deep breath. "So that brings me to my next apology. Ryan, I am SO sorry for cutting you out of my life for the past month."

The silence lingers between us for a moment. I know she has more to say, and I'm not in a rush. Finally, she lets out a nervous breath and continues, "I went through a lot of things emotionally that night. Ashton really screwed me up when I found out he was engaged to my step-sister, but that night he broke me like I've never been broken before. I walked the entire city until well after the sun had come up, questioning every decision I've ever made, and ultimately coming to the conclusion that I needed space from you – because in that moment I was fully convinced that I was a hindrance to you and your career, and that you would be better off without me."

"You know how crazy that sounds, right?" I ask her, turning into my neighborhood.

"At that time, no, I didn't." She stares at me. "He convinced me that I wasn't deserving of love, and that you'd end up leaving me anyway. So I decided that in order to help myself heal, and to protect myself and you in the future, I needed to end things."

I pull into the driveway and quickly throw the car into park. "That's *insane*, Brenna." I turn in my seat to face her. She looks so tiny and beautiful in the seat next to me, her face outlined by the streetlights. "I wanted to be there for you so badly. More than you will ever know. But you wouldn't let me."

"I know, and I'm sorry for that." Her eyes glisten with tears. "In hindsight, I wish I wouldn't have ran away from you, but what's done is done. I can only ask for your forgiveness now, and hope that you'll still want to be part of my life going forward."

Slowly, I reach out and take her hand in mine, our eyes locked. I know that she did what she felt she needed to do, even though it hurt both of us, but it truly sounds like she's taken responsibility for it. How could I not forgive her?

"Of course. I'm not going anywhere," I tell her. She smiles that radiant smile I've been missing, and I lean forward to capture her in a kiss, but she pulls away before my lips can touch hers.

"We still need to discuss Sam."

My chest tightens, my already crazy emotions gripping my heart even harder. "Yes. We do," I finally manage to say. "Um, lets go inside. It'll be easier and more comfortable than sitting out here in my car."

We head into the house. I leave my gear bag in the foyer and grab us each a bottle of water from the refrigerator. Then I take Brenna by the hand and lead her to one of the spare bedrooms, where boxes are stacked everywhere, still waiting to be unpacked.

We settle on the plush carpet in the middle of the room and I open one of the boxes. I know that at the top of this box is a photo of Sam and me. It's one of my most prized possessions.

"I have a confession," she says. I pause, hand still in the box. "The photo you're about to show me... I've already seen it." She squirms and sighs. "I was poking around your house one day and found it. But I trusted that one day you'd explain it to me, so I never asked. I'm sorry for not telling you before now."

I could choose to be angry, but I don't. Instead, I give the photo to her, placing it gently in her delicate hands. "I appreciate your honesty. There's a lot we weren't ready to share with each other, but now it's time."

We both look down at the photo of two smiling Canadian boys, both innocent and full of life. It feels like a lifetime ago. "This is my older brother, Sam. Skating came as naturally as breathing to him. He loved monster trucks, and pistachio ice cream, but most of all he loved the sport of hockey. He was my best friend and my hero."

"You look so much like him," she muses, smiling softly. "You must have been devastated when..."

"Yeah," is all I can say. We sit quietly for a moment, both lost in our thoughts. "Sam would have been the next Gretzky, I'm sure of it. He was amazing." I reach back into the box and, after a bit of digging, pull out another photo. I hand it to Brenna and she breathes in sharply. "This was my mother, Daisy."

"And I thought you and Sam looked a lot alike. You are the spitting image of your mom." Her hair is in those crazy late-eighties curls and I'm pretty sure she's wearing a windbreaker, but no other photo captures my mother so perfectly. My father is behind her, his arms wrapped around her waist, and their smiles radiate straight off the paper. She looks so peaceful, so free.

"My childhood was normal and wonderful. My parents were crazy about each other, Sam and I were fed and cared for and loved. My dad pushed Sam and I a little hard at times, but he knew we had the potential to make it big and I believe he had our best interests at heart. But when Sam died... everything changed."

I pull another photo out of the box. "This is the last photo I have of my mom. After Sam died, she completely withdrew from the world. She wouldn't come out of the bedroom, wouldn't eat, couldn't sleep... she was completely different."

We both look down at the photo in my hands. My once beautiful mother is a stranger, her entire body emaciated, nothing left but hollow cheeks and vacant eyes. She's at the window seat in her bedroom, head resting against the glass overlooking the lake where she lost her oldest son. I stole the moment in secret, capturing the photo before saying goodbye to her for what would, unbeknownst to either of us, end up being the last time.

"My father became... a monster. He went from being the kind of dad who would take a day off work just to go fishing with you, into one that never laughed or smiled or even said he was proud of me anymore. His training practices probably bordered on torture, but who was I to say? I was just a twelve year old kid who lost his best friend and both parents at the same time. So I pushed myself to be as good as Sam – to be the player he wasn't able to be. I was drafted, and left Toronto for Philadelphia. And I never looked back."

Brenna rests her hand on my knee.

"A couple years later, Mom died of a heart attack. At least, that's what it says on paper. But I truly believe she slowly died, over the course of several years, from a broken heart." I exhale through my nose, quelling the emotion threatening to bubble out of me. "I should have been there for her more, but I didn't know how. I don't know if it would have done any good or not, but I regret leaving her there with my father."

"You handled your grief, and her grief, and your father's grief as best as you could," Brenna says. She moves her hand from my knee and finds my hand instead, giving it a light squeeze. "You're only one person, Ryan. And one person can't save everyone, no matter how hard they try. You did what you needed to do to grow and heal and become the amazing person you are today. You have survived each and every attempt by your father to cut you down and destroy you, and yet you've also handled interactions with him with dignity and a grace that he hasn't earned yet you freely give. And you know what? I'm *positive* that your mom and Sam are both looking down on you and they're so proud of you and all that you've accomplished in life."

I don't know when they started, but a couple tears slide down my cheeks. "Thank you. You're too good to me."

"I could say the same for you." She absently brushes the pad of her thumb across the back of my hand. "Thank you for sharing that with me. A lot of things make a lot more sense now - like why you were so messed up when your dad came to town."

"Thankfully, he only drops by once a year, which is one time too many," I say gruffly. "He's such an asshole, but he's still my father, you know? I try to keep myself in that happy medium of caring about him as my father but keeping enough distance for my own health and safety, but it isn't easy. I've taken a lot of shit over the years from friends and family who think that me cutting him out of my life is selfish and wrong. I had to cut those people out of my life, too."

"Only you can know what's best for you," she says thoughtfully. "I think it's brave to make a decision like that, even when it's in your best interest.

I feel my cheeks warm. "Thank you." We stare at each other. She leans in, close, her breath a whisper on my cheek. Neither of us move, uncertain of what to do next.

"So... what does this mean for us?" she finally asks.

"I'm not going to sugarcoat anything," I tell her. "I've missed you, Brenna. So fucking much. But I think you already know that."

She squirms a bit. "I figured, but once you stopped trying to contact me... I wasn't sure... if maybe you'd changed your mind, moved on from me."

It kills me that she would think I could move on from her so fast. "There hasn't been anyone else. Even after our game in Edmonton when a couple of the guys tried to hook me up with a puck bunny." Her eyes widen and I quickly continue before she can jump to conclusions. "That night I locked myself in the hotel room and did nothing but think about you. I can't even try to picture myself with another woman because every time I close my eyes, all I see is you. Every time I breathe, all I can smell is you. It has taken everything within me to not contact you at all for these past few weeks. I didn't move on because I *can't* just go and move on from you." The words are out of my mouth before I can stop them. "I love you."

Everything stops as what I've said processes for both of us. I've filleted my heart and laid it out onto a platter for this girl. I'm scared shitless waiting for her to say something. Thankfully, her cheeks flush as a smile spreads across her face. "I love you too."

Our lips meet, and I know I've found peace... happiness... home.

EPILOGUE

"That's the last of it," John says, closing the front door behind us. I trudge across the snowy sidewalk to my car, squeezing the box in my arms into the backseat with the others before shutting the door. I turn to look back at the house I've lived in with Carly for the last several years and shiver in the winter air. Carly and John are looking at the house as well as we all lose ourselves in a few moments of memories shared in this place.

"So this is it," Carly finally says.

"This is it," I echo.

We hug each other as tightly as two girls in giant poofy winter coats are able. Their wedding is only a month away, and Ryan closed on his house this week, so it made sense for us to both move out now rather than wait any longer.

"I'll call you every day," I tell her earnestly.

"Of course you will, silly," she says with a grin. "Or else we'd both go crazy."

I give John a hug. "Take care of my girl, okay?"

"Always," he replies.

We say our goodbyes and I hop into my car. With one last glance at the tiny dump I've called home for the past few years, I drive away and head toward Ryan's new house in the suburbs.

The last several months have been wonderful. One of the first things Ryan did after we reconciled was to hire a lawyer for me to get a restraining order against Ashton. I didn't want to believe it was necessary, but Jane agreed that separating ourselves from him as much as possible would be best. Not that I'd ever go back to him. I've loved and nearly lost it all because of Ashton. I won't make that same mistake again.

My father reached out to me around Christmastime to try to make amends. With guidance from Jane and lots of support from Ryan, my dad and I have been having weekly phone calls and are slowly rebuilding our relationship. I'm still not ready to talk to his wife or my step-sister, and that's okay. I know it will take time, and I'm in no rush.

Ryan has been completely killing it on the ice. He's been having his best season in several years. Playing on the first line with his friend Nils and Morgan's brother Patrick seems to work well for him, and I now know what the term "first line" even means. Between Ryan, Carly, and Morgan, I'm turning into quite the hockey buff.

Ryan took me on vacation to Cabo during the All-Star break last month. Apparently every year each team gets a break built into their schedule as sort of a mid-season vacation. I spent so much time on the beach and got insanely sunburnt, and it was wonderful. Of course, a ton of photos of Ryan and I ended up on the blog sites, but most of them have finally stopped calling me a bunny and now refer to me as Ryan's girlfriend instead.

Ashton did a lot of damage to me that has been difficult to unravel, much like the pain Ryan's father caused him has been something we've had to work through as well. However, we've been growing closer to each other, and I feel myself healing, slowly but surely. When Ryan looks at me, it's as if I'm the only girl in the entire city. He works very hard to show me he loves me in every way possible, and his patience in the difficult times has been a blessing.

In addition to asking me to move in with him, Ryan also went behind my back and paid off *all* of my credit cards and student loans. I didn't know he did it until I went to pay one of them and the company told me I had a zero balance on my account.

At first, I was livid - how dare he pity me and secretly throw money my way? And then I realized what a blessing it was - because I was starting to receive default notices on all of them. He told me that he did it because he knew I was killing myself trying to stay afloat, and he hated to see me suffer so much over something he could change so easily.

With the debts gone, I was finally able to stop taking on so many side-jobs at my normal job and focus more on the quality of my work. Of course, now Ryan knows to ask me before he does something ridiculous and crazy like that again, but he also knows what an incredible gift he gave me with that simple - to him - act of generosity.

I'm so incredibly thankful that I have him in my life.

I pull into my parking spot in the garage of the mansion Ryan purchased. Okay, so maybe mansion is a stretch, but it's certainly bigger than one person could ever need. I grab one of the boxes out of the backseat and head inside.

"Honey, I'm home!" I call out in as sing-songish of a voice as I can muster before bursting into giggles. My voice echoes through the front half of the house and is met with silence. I set the box down on the kitchen counter and kick the shut the door behind me as I take off my gloves and coat. "Ryan?"

He's supposed to be here, unpacking. I trek through the kitchen and round the corner to the living room where I am met with a hundred white balloons floating around the room. Ryan is standing in the middle of it all and, as soon as I walk in, he drops to one knee. I feel my breath catch in my throat.

"Brenna Lynn Wilson, will you move in with me?" he asks me, opening a ring box to reveal a key to the house perched inside of it. I exhale the breath I was holding and laugh.

"Ryan! I already agreed to move in with you, you dork."

"Oh, yeah," he says, scratching his head with his free hand. Then he reaches into his pocket and pulls out a ring. My heart stops. "I guess that just leaves this other question I had: Brenna Lynn Wilson, will you marry me?"

"Yes," I say, the words strangled in a sob as my eyes fill with tears. I rush to Ryan and he captures me in a hug, spinning me in a circle around the room. "Of course I'll marry you."

"I love you so fucking much," Ryan says in my ear.

"I love you too," I say through happy tears. He finally releases me, grabbing my hand and sliding the ring onto my finger. The center stone is a large, pale blue aquamarine, the exact same color as Ryan's eyes, surrounded by tiny white diamonds.

"Ryan, this ring is so beautiful," I say breathlessly.

"Do you like it?" he asks, his tone giddy. "I had it custom made just for you. I hoped it wasn't too much."

I stare at the ring gracing my hand and smile. "It's perfect."

I may never in a thousand years feel like I deserve this man and the life we are building together, but he chose me, and he chooses me over and over, every single day. And of course, I choose him.

Overcome with emotion, I impulsively pull my shirt up and over my head, throwing it to the floor. My eyes find Ryan's, searching their crystalline depths, as I place his hands on my bare skin. He watches me carefully, a smile tugging at the edges of his lips.

In the lowest, quietest, most husky voice I can muster, I beg him, "Please, fuck me."

I don't have to tell him twice.

THANKS

To my husband Allen, for introducing me to hockey in the first place, and for being supportive of this crazy little adventure (and all the other crazy little adventures both past and future). I love you.

To Jessica, Morgan, Elizabeth, Sandra, Lara, Katherine, Taylor, Adrienne, Kat, Lauren, Melinda, Jami, Lona, Jonathan, and anyone else who listened to me talk about this book, let me bounce ideas off of them, proofread early manuscripts, or encouraged me not to give up writing it. I couldn't have done it without you all!

ABOUT THE AUTHOR

Abby Burch had never even seen an NHL game until the Red Wings were in the Stanley Cup Playoffs in 2013. Even though they were eliminated in the Semifinals, Abby was hooked. She attended her first game for her birthday in the 2013-2014 season.

When she isn't cheering for the Red Wings or Golden Knights, Abby enjoys running her wedding photography business, traveling, watching videos of other people playing video games, running in 5K races, and being an advocate for type 1 diabetes awareness, a condition which she was diagnosed with in 2012.

You can find more of Abby at her diabetes blog, photograbetic.wordpress.com, and on her wedding photography website, lewayneproductions.com.

Made in the USA
Middletown, DE
29 December 2022

18420167R00106